THE NEW EXISTENCE

THE NEW EXISTENCE

Michael Collins

UNIVERSITY OF IOWA PRESS | IOWA CITY

University of Iowa Press, Iowa City 52242
Copyright © 2021 by Michael Collins
uipress.uiowa.edu
Printed in the United States of America

Text design by April Leidig
Cover design by Erin Kirk New

Printed on acid-free paper

Library of Congress Cataloging-in-Publication Data
Names: Collins, Michael, 1964– author.
Title: The New Existence / Michael Collins.
Description: Iowa City: University of Iowa Press, [2021] |
Identifiers: LCCN 2021004313 (print) | LCCN 2021004314 (ebook) |
ISBN 9781609387969 (paperback) | ISBN 9781609387976 (ebook)
Classification: LCC PR6053.O4263 N49 2021 (print) |
LCC PR6053.O4263 (ebook) | DDC 823/.914—dc23
LC record available at https://lccn.loc.gov/2021004313
LC ebook record available at https://lccn.loc.gov/2021004314

PART I

The greatest hazard, losing one's self, can occur
very quietly in the world, as if it were nothing at all.
—SØREN KIERKEGAARD

One

I T H A D B E E N O V E R a decade since Helen Price had driven along the Gold Coast during the push of an early afternoon commute. This time, however, she was driving against the flow of traffic, heading in and not out toward the suburbs. It sat as a point of significance, figuring in the literal transformation of her life these past few years against the grain of any true forward momentum, a life pushing backward in time, toward old memories, to islands of remembrance now assembling as the history of who she was or who she had once been.

How had it come to pass, this sweeping change, this passage of time, when she found herself at a point where life appeared not here or there but somewhere in a remote past? Maybe it was the melancholy essence of growing old.

T H E R E W A S A N H O U R T O G O before her doctor's appointment. Yet Helen couldn't help but weigh the significance of a receptionist's insistence to reschedule from Monday to Friday her appointment with Dr. Marchant, and at his downtown office, where, allegedly, a last-minute cancellation had opened in the late afternoon, the concatenation of facts hemming her into a reality that there could be no further happiness, no further life.

Helen considered staying on Lake Shore Drive but then exited on Michigan Avenue, feeling an immediate sense of déjà vu. She had taken this route so many times before. It was not, however, quite as it had been. Nothing was anymore. If she could alter now the perspective, if such things were possible, if she could beg such small mercies, reclaim the past, she would adjust, first, the size of her car, give it a grander, more stylized dimension, swap her compact Corolla for one of those bygone, tail-finned floating Detroit fortresses. She had in mind the '61 Buick 4600 Invicta, purchased the first year of their marriage: the Invicta, the first and last car she ever drove right off a showroom floor.

And on this melancholy day, in seeking a point of past connectedness, she would adjust, too, the garish fluorescence of Michigan Avenue storefronts, temper them with the Technicolor warmth of *Breakfast at Tiffany's*, filter everything through a Hollywood cheesecloth that had defined an America of pillbox hats and high heels. How one appeared to the world had mattered once upon a time. And if she could affect those changes, alter life slightly, she would undo so many things, find that point of reentry into life when she had the thread of things. She would reinstate the shah of Iran, unhood the American hostages, send Khomeini back into exile. She would reinstall Nixon, unplug the Watergate devices, silence Deep Throat, undo Nixon's visit to Red China. She would fill the empty gas pumps of the 1973 oil embargo, reinstitute the monopoly of Bethlehem Steel, resanctify the unions, resurrect Jimmy Hoffa. She would lead a retreat out of Vietnam, dislodge the bullets from the brains of MLK, Bobby and John F. Kennedy, consign to obscurity Sirhan Sirhan, Jack Ruby, and Lee Harvey Oswald. She'd repeal, too, the Marshall Plan, spin back time to a preadolescence of first cognition, stop time somewhere after the dropping of the bombs on Hiroshima and Nagasaki, begin it again in the Cold War brinksmanship with the defined enemy of the Soviet Union.

She was aware she had not included undoing the recent horrors of 9/11. It was not her history. She felt the emotional slippage, the piling of new histories that no longer impinged on her immediate life, just as untold tens of millions before her must have surely arrived at certain points where events as monumental as Pearl Harbor or the Black Monday of the Great Depression just floated, unmoored from any real significance, psychological life lived not in a forward trajectory but built around points of personal perspective, each generation—no, each individual—an island unto itself.

Helen was conscious of how upset her son, Norman, would be in her expressing such sentiment. Undoubtedly, he would have stridently argued against her lament for a succession of generations who had slaughtered themselves across a half century of two world wars. She could almost hear Norman's voice in her head, his injurious assessment of other people's lives that had coalesced in his hurtful one-man shows, *Confessions of a Latchkey Kid* and *Angry Man,* the latter a scathing indictment of her husband Walter's career that became a minor Chicago theatrical hit. How would Norman now title her life—*Dying Woman*? She imagined the exchange, her offstage voice playing against Norman's, this the endgame, the pitiless verdict of a son against his parents, against two people who had gone broke educating what turned out to be a recalcitrant gay man who had decided to damn the history of civilization. She felt her heart race. The estrangement was Norman's, though she was willing to cede his was a revisionist history now taught in schools, a history that gave him his confidence, his optimism, and his distrust of all things past.

TIME WAS RUNNING OUT for Helen Price. She felt her eyes well. She thought of how the end had started, the nadir of a strip-mall Red Lobster dinner over Thanksgiving, an experience so unsettling it had set her and Walter on the high seas a month later for a Christmas Caribbean cruise ultimately overshadowed by a salmonella outbreak. It was the persistence of stomach pains in the months after that had suggested all was not well. Cancer was in her uterus and then her lungs.

She found her eyes blurring, the entire cruise fiasco opening up again, the medevac rescue efforts off the coast of Saint Croix, a quotient of elderly helicoptered to an island hospital for precautionary reasons, her included, and against her better judgment, where a month later, she discovered, travel insurance had not covered the six-minute airlift, the medevac outfit billing her credit card eleven thousand dollars she was still disputing.

SNOW HAD THREATENED and now fell in drifting flakes. She should have turned toward Dr. Marchant. Instead, she turned east on Jackson, followed the river's contour, lost in an elongated fall of shadows, passed gelled bars of afternoon light intersecting the East/West streets in a roll call of presidential names—Washington, Madison, Monroe, and

Adams. Then she turned east again toward the lake on Jackson, crossing Franklin until she passed the intersection of La Salle, where she had worked until 1992, the ground zero of her existence.

She craned forward. Above her, two hooded figures atop the Mercantile Exchange—an Egyptian grasping a sheaf of wheat and a Native American holding an ear of corn—time here arrested, the Exchange and the Federal Reserve Bank harkening to a bygone age of all things tangible, to a time when the nation's wealth was tied to the gold standard. Helen was willing to admit her own failings. It was just her perception, her way of seeing the world, and yet she felt a need to defend herself. No, nothing made sense anymore. Not really. She whispered the name Theodore Feldman, the name an incantation, Theodore Feldman, decorated veteran of World War II who had called the Japanese "Japs," his one betrayal to time spent in the Pacific carnage. Where had men like that gone, men of means, valor, and material substance?

It existed in her mind, the gurgle of the water cooler serviced by a Culligan Man in a dickey bow and hitched polio limp passed off as a war injury, Helen opening the mail with a dagger of a letter opener, screening all calls for Mr. Feldman until he buzzed and called her in, whereafter she spent the greater part of her day transcribing, pen and pad in hand.

She could almost smell his aftershave. The speeches he spent days preparing for the trustees, circumscribing points of business, landing upon the overall challenges, but so, too, the opportunities—remarks that inspired board members to nod approvingly amidst considerations concerning drinks elsewhere. Mr. Feldman, in the waning lunch hour, placing a jocular call to the office to ensure "it hadn't burned down!"— a remark that always made her flush. On these occasions, Helen hearing the raspy scratch of Mr. Feldman's five o'clock growth and clink of plates being gathered from the impressive spread of tables, a hubbub of corporate entitlement that made her feel all was well, that everything that mattered was in the capable hands of irreproachable men of character and moral judgment. She would never, *ever* have thought that Mr. Theodore Feldman would bow out, stepping from his office window atop the Chicago skyline on Black Monday 1987, but he did. That was when her life most surely ended, or so said Norman in the years afterward, implying improprieties of a most sordid sort, pressing against her loyalty and fond remembrance of Mr. Feldman with his general cynicism of all things past.

THERE WAS THE SENSE it was over now, yet Helen resisted the final act, her thoughts again with Mr. Feldman. Not long before his death, he purchased a video recorder, and taking her into his confidence, pointed to the Board of Trade, to a statue of Ceres, goddess of crops. What he liked, the connective sense of pagan ritual tied to human life, the ancients with their pantheon of gods—Zeus, god of thunder; Athena, goddess of wisdom; Apollo, god of knowledge; Aphrodite, goddess of love—the apportioned rite of complex emotions, what he called "the top-down management style of the Greeks!"

What she remembered, the sinewy quality of his body, how it gave off a faint smell of metabolized bourbon and nicotine, both of them staring across at the Mercantile Exchange, trading in the breadbasket bounty of the Great Plains, never mind the history of the Okies, or what an underhanded proposition progress was when looked at closely. Mr. Feldman winked in saying things like that, as though she understood. She didn't. She had not read *The Grapes of Wrath*. She tried and never finished, though she saw the movie. Mr. Feldman changed her by degrees. Helen sniffled. She imagined Mr. Feldman in a liberal pouring of a midmorning splash of soda and dash of scotch, Mr. Feldman smoking in deep pulls, a smokiness that blued the air, so he could be seen waving his way out as though come from a distant front.

She believed it, the chiseled jaw of a man who had been willing to give his life, his youth, his virility, so others might live. She would do anything for a man like that. There was no humiliation, no dishonor in her acts. She would not be dissuaded by alternative truths. She was outside the feminist debate of principled ideals. They had no idea what storms could blow in the heart. You found those landings of the self, your wants, only in the respite of a hard-gained ceasefire, in an armistice of blood and death. It took nothing from her life to have listened to him, to have loved him. There, it was *said*!

HELEN CIRCLED AGAIN her former life, passed the burnished brass revolving door of her old office building. She wanted to go deeper, find that place where it all still existed, the time before her illness, before that godforsaken 9/11, before the accumulation of joys and regrets that had somehow rubbed out her significance.

She felt a rushing sense of grief. How to configure time, reassemble one's history, land upon that moment when hope failed, when promise died? And did it matter? Did it really? But it did. This was the past receding, the decoupling of a life force.

It was decided. She felt a control she had not felt in a long time. Yes, that most surely was it, why she had come here one last time. To reclaim the feelings of those years of comfort in what had been back then, the incalculability of life in an emerging modern world of options as she had continued to work after marriage, and *even* after Norman's birth, the surrogate infrastructure of daycare overseen by attentive professionals in child psychology, all vastly more equipped to nurture growth than any mother sequestered with a child and a TV in the doldrums of the midafternoon soaps. How forward-looking it had all seemed, the delegation of tasks per one's merits, one's interests, the uncompromising vision that everyone could have everything one needed, or at least the opportunity to seek it. And now it was gone.

She had such fond memories, the morning hustle to get Norman to the school bus, leaving the utilitarian suburb of a modest house in a car financed on affordable down payments for the throng on the commuter train platform. She remembered it all with absolute clarity, parking her car amidst the gleam of other new cars, proceeding in the push of life, venturing toward the ceiling frescos beyond the revolving door of her office building. She could see in her mind's eye the topaz and onyx mosaics in the building's lobby, the pageant of midwestern history captured in a series of mosaics, the collective first landings rendered in a two-dimensional flatness suggesting an uncomplicated arrangement of bringing a Christian God to the natives; a sharing of gifts between frocked French missionaries, Bibles in hand, olive-skinned natives in ceremonial headdress offering a peace pipe at some appointed canoe portage. No matter the real history. She could hear Norman in her head shouting, and she wanted to scream at him, for who *now* didn't know the true history! "Yes, Norman, the ravages of smallpox and measles, the internment of natives and the Trail of Tears . . . I *know* . . . I *know* . . . you are so *damned* right . . . ," and yet it was in these first landings, these exchanges, that the glory of a new world was founded—from a humble barter of animal pelts to the glorious reach of skyscrapers in a span of mere centuries. No *single* history could account for such progress. It was all too vastly complicated and yet so manifestly literal, and it had all come together once upon a time, the perfect inning, the improbable no-hitter of American dominance, and all of it had coincided with her youth.

ON THE SEAT beside her lay a letter from the state attorney's office, an official subpoena requiring Walter's testimony in a case she'd thought long closed, reopened under the provisions of the Patriot Act, alleging Walter's criminal obstruction of justice and active involvement in the planned execution of two gangland dealers who had been set to testify against members of Chicago's South Side drug unit.

Helen was suddenly crying, her thoughts settled on Norman, on his *Angry Man* show, on the quiet indictment of a fiction that might yet be appraised as fact, as evidence. What would he *say* about them, about her and about Walter, about *their lives*? She ran the back of her hand under her nose, tasting her own tears, drifting in the blurred flow of traffic.

The subpoena was a week old. She had uncovered it in Walter's sock drawer, rifling through his known hiding places following the stiff formality of a message that had been left on her answering machine by an attorney with a voice not unlike Norman's, which, in the swoon of medication, she had first mistaken as Norman's. There had been, too, a call from Walter's legal counsel, Mr. Ahmet, who had then appeared at her home for fear of a wiretap, banging on her door, which she had refused to open. Life had gotten away from her, all of it.

Reaching into her purse, Helen retrieved her pills. Tipping her head, she felt the reflexive gag of self-preservation, though she managed to swallow all of them, the effect immediate in the sudden euphoria of knowing how it would end.

TIME SLOWED. Snow fell, the city disappeared, Helen deep in the processional crawl of an evening commute. She was suddenly so very, *very* tired. In the corridor of her funneling exit, she edged parallel with a desolate Grant Park, vaguely aware of the wail of a siren, a sound hard to pinpoint against the tumbling end-over-end effect of the pills.

Blue strobe police lights cut the slate grey of wet falling snow. In her rearview mirror, Helen saw something she had long ago outrun stalking her still. It was time. Closing her eyes, she crossed all six lanes of Lake Shore Drive, beyond, the grey cradling of Lake Michigan like a vast subconscious stirring.

Two

WALTER PRICE gripped the steering wheel of his Impala in the sluggish commute of a Friday afternoon under threat of early snow. He knew the union snowplow drivers at the city depots were catching a last shut-eye before the night assault on the city. In the coming winter months, hundreds of thousands of tons of salt would be spread to keep Chicago running. Where else did a people stand against the forces of nature, when there were sunbaked paradises like Miami, Fort Lauderdale, Dallas, and Tempe within a two-day journey? It said something profound about Chicago. It spoke to its blunt stubbornness, its marauding physicality, its sentinel scrapers, among the world's tallest, facing down the cold knife of the Arctic. More so than any other city, the charge of its elders, its mayor, was a task as prophetic as any Old Testament miracle, as miraculous as Moses parting the Red Sea, perhaps even greater. No one man could face down the onslaught of a Chicago winter.

Walter felt a deep pride in being associated with the municipal presence of what was left of the Chicago machine, the dull throb of its power waiting to roll and begin its work. It gave him a feeling of belonging, a sense of collective identity—a feeling that set him apart from how American life was now lived.

In fact, in these later years of his career, in the outing of political corruption, in the half decade of post 9/11 Patriot Act scrutiny and the rise of Homeland Security, he felt the shift of zealous righteousness, routing out not so much terrorism as an older system of political governance, undoing what had existed for so long, enabling agencies, armed with new powers, to avenge old political vendettas. This, in his humble estimation, was the true legacy of the felling of the Twin Towers, the encroaching power of government wresting and centralizing power under its own agency. Such thoughts made Walter feel old, older than his sixty-six years might have suggested.

Like so many others caught up in Chicago's political machine, his life had been manacled to an intractable union. He was used to the union controlling tactics, the blue flu protests and general worker go-slows, along with the collective bargaining stranglehold of seasoned union negotiators, all this union muscle coalescing around an institutional mediocrity based on cronyism, nepotism, and seniority over merit.

From the outside looking in, it was nothing he would have endorsed, but from within, it defined a hard-fought dignity against historical realities of what happened when you became disenfranchised. It was a matter of principle, but more importantly, *survival*. He understood his beloved Chicago as something other than New York or Los Angeles, knew it as the great absorber of mongrel immigrant waves; first the Irish; then the Eastern Bloc refugees, potato-faced giants, monsters of the midway, all in long coats and fur hats, not so much seeking fortunes as escaping the ravages of famines, pogroms, and genocide. It made those who arrived in Chicago a different breed, hard, suspicious, and provincial. There was no real American Dream here, not in the way it was espoused elsewhere. In his heart, he knew that this was what gave Chicago its essence, its physicality and presence. He was sure that, without Chicago, there would be no America, his hometown existing in that convergent space between dreams and reality.

At times through his midcareer, listening to the nightly news regarding the occasional resurfacing of ex-Nazi prison guards in a Detroit or Cleveland auto plant, he understood why the discoveries were never made in Daytona Beach or Miami, the ex-guards inhabiting the vast anonymity of the steel and car manufacturing plants, the grim work-a-day cities subsuming histories—mundane, horrific, or otherwise—where, in the quieting hours, jaded men drank in the rumbling lanes of local bowling alleys, the pins arranged like a consortium of dissidents before a firing squad.

"Piss nobody off" was the general rule for anybody working within the machine of municipal Chicago. Don't distinguish yourself in any appreciable way other than to subtly broadcast a willingness to overlook staring too deeply into the entanglement of all things political. Over his working lifetime, he had become acculturated to looking the other way from systemic political patronage and racketeering, the skimming from state and federal dollars through shell companies and phantom workers on streets and sanitation awarded contracts, fraud orchestrated and controlled through a tight network of political gamesmanship, a political glad-handing and exchanging of brown envelope kickbacks in back office deals. The means justified the end in Chicago politics, partisan gerrymandering thwarting judicial oversight, the spoils of state and federal dollars divvied according to rapacious self-interest, opportunism, personal charisma, and maybe well-intentioned political will, *one hoped*, but in the end, it came down to a money grab bordering on or crossing over into outright criminality in most cases.

He had witnessed it all in his career, the exodus and return of money interests from the city center in the sixties, the construction of the ill-conceived high-rise ghettoes in the wasteland of white flight on the South Side, then the reclamation and regentrification of the ghetto lands in the early nineties, rezoning ordinances pushed through the courts, legal challenges dismissed by bought judges, the arbitrary application of the law suddenly enforced where it hadn't been, a racial divide persisting, if one looked deep enough, connected to the Civil War, to the great tidal waves of the unshackled who, in rising out of the Deep South, in the promise of Lincoln and emancipation, had resettled in the industrial rim of the Great Lakes, so it was understood that this was what the prospect of freedom really looked like, and that the killing fields of Shiloh, Antietam, and Gettysburg had only dislodged and shifted a greater discontent into the North.

But there was also a different side to Chicago, a side he loved, which had sustained his general faith in the city and God. For so many years he had traveled the divide between the shifting ethnic influences, Chicago morph, the slow trickle of immigrant peasant Ukrainians, Poles, Russian Jews, and Armenians, denizens of forgotten villages in the Ural and Carpathian Mountains coming to American shores, for this was a city people still whispered about, this city on the plains a beacon, holding out a dream.

What Walter had learned along the way was neither to judge himself nor others too harshly, to tuck away a small trove of mercies against the general flow of days in his line of duty, to take solace in the *Eyewitness News* story about the recovery of a baby from a dumpster who would miraculously make it, the shot kid on the subway who would walk again, the slashed college model whose reconstructive cosmetic surgery was donated by an upscale Jewish plastic surgeon, to the small moments of passing beauty he witnessed from the front seat of his unmarked car, those events that never made the nightly news; the processional grandeur of spring Saturday mornings up by Loyola, small veiled Mexican handmaidens making their first communion, appearing in virginal white and patent leather shoes, daughters of dealers and the ordinary alike.

In his heart he believed in the goodness of mankind. It was just the day-to-day details you had to overlook, that other law that justified his own participation in petty bribes and protection rackets. Not all violence was senseless, not all corruption necessarily bad—his sense of physical presence and menace needed at times to subtly reinforce new boundaries, force the retreat of drug gangs from advancing ethnic neighborhoods, push back the virus of the perpetuated welfare state of Medicare and food stamp programs. If it took pistol-whipping a thug or shaking down a new establishment for protection, that was ultimately the price of freedom in its truest sense, the measured response in equal proportion to the apparent threat. There were actions and compromises that could never be negotiated or arbitrated in the light of day. It took men like Walter to do what was necessary, to lay down the groundwork, which, more often than not, led to real progress, legitimized eventually in the veneer of some political deal and ribbon-cutting ceremony at the renaming of a street.

WALTER PUT A HAND to his face, pulled at the tiredness in the bags beneath his eyes. At some point he had grown old. He was privy to preliminary interviews of old witnesses already called in deals orchestrated through leaks to set everyone on edge. He held the steering wheel, his hands tightening in the subconscious formulation of a defense, some statement of his own history and his city's past.

The great Chicago machine was grinding to a halt, Walter reconciled to its passing. What could be uncovered that wasn't already known or at least intuited? What purpose did these grand jury investigations really serve? At times, he thought the assault on the machine, his beloved Chicago, analogous to the choppy satellite footage released by the military from the predatory drones that dominated the cable news coverage, the shock and awe of weaponry controlled from bunkers in Nevada tens of thousands of miles away, auguring a divestment of real interest. Innocent collateral damage discounted, the probing powers of the Patriot Act, the post-9/11 hysteria uncovering a flawed, human corruption that for so long had existed out in the open, or, if not exactly out in the open, at least accepted by all parties concerned, for that was how the machine had held together once upon a time in the brokering of human failings and human hopes.

In truth, his preoccupation lay elsewhere. He understood there would be no last grandstand, nothing but a shuffling appearance before the grand jury, a guarded account of what he knew, trying to conceal his original perjury, revealing little but a confounding sense of a forgetfulness of days and events, relying on his age, his infirmity.

WALTER HAD BEGUN tailing Helen coming off Sheridan Road, down through Loyola and onto Lake Shore Drive, expecting her progress toward Dr. Marchant's office. He planned, like a stakeout, to be there upon her exit in the clinical corridor of the hospital, leading her for coffee in an antiseptic cafeteria basement, and *yes*, telling her about the indictment, laying out the measure of their lives.

She was dying, and yet there were issues between them never settled. The first, in retrospect petty, Helen's having had to produce her birth certificate at their civil union, where it was revealed that she was five years older than she had admitted. There had been tears, and all because a clerk had joked how Helen had caught herself a younger man. Once revealed, it laid bare what Walter had suspected, that Helen had a past. He was settled on her beginning an explanation, open to a broad appeal that she loved him. And yet she didn't explain. It was so suddenly apparent that she would cede nothing.

As time passed, and with it the inevitable emergence of Mr. Feldman, he came to view the divine providence of Helen as something akin to a *Twilight Zone* episode, where there was always a price to be exacted for unsuspecting fortune.

He let the truth settle, struck by the sullen reality that he had proved ineffectual in commanding her attention, her love. She needed him to a point, then didn't. It was something long ago reconciled, the power of Mr. Feldman, the falter and collapse of a marriage. There was a point when such realities settled as unalterable reality, Walter understanding or rationalizing that they were both victims, that what he lost, Helen never gained, not really, Mr. Feldman the consummate coward, leaving her behind.

AMIDST THE crosstown crawl of the late afternoon commute, Walter turned on his siren. He wanted Helen to pull over. He was ready to exit his car as though this was an ordinary traffic stop, to approach and confront her. He saw the look in her eyes in her rearview mirror, the recognition, and then Helen did what she had done so often, escaped him, crossing all six lanes of Lake Shore Drive before plunging into the depths of Lake Michigan.

Three

T HE INDECIPHERABLE babble of a Chinese CD played down a long hallway as Norman Price sat staring into the charcoal grey of a developing morning. It was not yet 7:30 A.M., and yet he had been writing for almost two hours, his writing life in sync with his partner Kenneth's five-thirty departure to a downtown Starbucks.

He lived now for this settling sense of accomplishment, these hours stolen into a lingering dark of fall mornings, the act of writing a clairvoyant mediation between the tugging undertow of the subconscious and an awakening unguarded consciousness. This, in his humble opinion, was where the essence of the soul hid, in the first stirring of things felt. He tried to rally toward this old routine, but in truth, he had accomplished little.

Something had changed within him. He stared into the hallway mirror at his daughter, Grace, or an image of her, reflected in another mirror, Grace, arranging her Barbies in military tribunal—the Barbies lined up outside a Victorian dollhouse guarded by a pair of salt-and-pepper-shaker Scottie dogs.

If Norman had one pressing regret, it was how things had changed in the two years since his daughter's adoption from China. He had consciously begun connecting a coldness settling over her to a latent survival instinct that she must have perfected in the way institutions such as the one she had been rescued from functioned on the absolute uniformity and anonymity of those they housed. Or perhaps he was overthinking it. Or just maybe all Chinese were like this, the billion faces so absolutely the same, if he could submit to such an idea without racist intent. It was hard deciding. Could he have done more? Perhaps . . . *Yes*. But then Grace never complained. There was no real issue. In her quietness, she let him work, and that was the most important determinant in Norman's life, how he compartmentalized his relationships, finding a diver's way into his own creative space. In truth, he liked the disembodied sense of remove, occasionally turning between sentences or midsentence, seeing her replicated image and not her physical presence, processing the mediating space between things seen and unseen, the flow of atoms or particles reconstituting her image, so she was there and not there.

What an improbable conundrum, existence! Grace touched things deep within him. He was glad she had come into his life. It fell as a revelation. Yes, he was better for her being in his life. He nodded in affirming it. In fact, it made him aware of how he had previously lived in the diminished company of a sullen, sad-eyed dog. "Shitter" was what he had called his dog toward the end, and not by its name, Bruce, which was an absurd name, extending beyond a reasonable expectation the sway a dog should have had over its master. Names were important for a writer. He learned it the hard way, in having to put Shitter down, in the imperative way real life worked out, which was always really the only way to see into the heart of matters. Yes, there were things Norman was not proud of doing. But that was life.

In truth, he hadn't had the money to prolong Shitter's life. It was less his callousness and more that there was the option of euthanizing, and he hadn't the money to pay for the procedure that might have extended Bruce's life, though, with the Shitter's head in his lap, Norman had steeled against his own lack of resources and asked, "How does the accused plead to the charge of repeatedly and knowingly shitting on the carpet?"

He was young then. Putting the question in such a way limited and extended his magnanimity at times. It was an exercise in his craft, shaping experience into Art. It made him less sanctimonious. He knew what he was capable of doing. He was not immune to self-reproach. He knew the dark secret that life could be stopped in an instant. Existence was not a given. There was, and then there was not. If anybody disagreed— "Just ask Bruce!"

It was a line used in *Reflections from a Futon*, a one-man act performed not long after Bruce's passing in the small black box theater in Chicago. He even made up a T-shirt with the phrase "Just ask Bruce!"—the philosophical effect of the act eclipsing the actuality of the sentence of death. People had not thought Bruce real, or they didn't want to know Bruce was real; Norman decided it was the latter. People actively subverted conscious thought all the time. It was a survival instinct, part of the process of laughter and forgetting.

Looking away from his computer, making new resolutions, Norman made a pledge to be more attentive, more caring with his daughter. They would get out more. They would take walks. They would do what normal people did, because there was valor and honor in the simple things in life.

NORMAN STARED INTO a sky the color of pearl. It was snowing in swirling flakes. Today, more so than any other, he was aware of the Chinese CD playing. How strange, this life, a writer submitting to a language he would never intuit, Chinese so unlike French or Spanish or any of the Romance languages that found their cadence in some shared linguistic past.

Of course, he could have tried to learn Chinese, but philosophically, he had decided against it, the linguistic distance ensuring his influence would be as unobtrusive as possible. What Grace brought of herself, her world, would remain intact. Principled ideas of autonomy, justice, and sovereign independence were important to Norman. Grace was the culminating achievement of normality he had sought so hard to achieve in a project dating back some six years to his relationship with Kenneth Birch.

Yes, he would have to give Kenneth credit for his involvement in what he had secured against life, this rescued child who would outlive him, Norman, aware how unartfully he had settled on Kenneth, overloading his conscious thoughts with Grace, when it was Kenneth he was really thinking about, for if there was ever a biography about Norman, and he dearly hoped there might be some day, it would necessarily detail Kenneth's influence on his life.

In the gathering light of early morning, as Norman turned from his work to prepare breakfast, he fell again on the attenuated series of early evening drinks with Kenneth and colleagues, how the evenings always ended with the inevitable parting kisses and hugs set against the ambient buzz of a throng with reservations for an eight or eight-thirty dinner, Norman shepherding Kenneth into the night air, the sudden quieting of a cab door shutting, signaling the night was over before it had ever really started. In its totality, it had been a staid, complicated, and yet quiet routine, a containment ultimately benefitting Norman, the reality always lingering that Kenneth, almost a decade younger, would not stay into the retiring years of Norman's own existence.

Now it was happening. Ten weeks earlier, while doing laundry, Norman found a phone number in a zipped inner compartment of Kenneth's gym bag along with a two-condom pack, one of the condoms disconcertingly missing, something so patently obvious. Didn't Kenneth know Norman would find the condoms doing the laundry, emptying Kenneth's gym bag, which he always did?

Writing down the phone number, Norman replaced the note alongside the condom pack, rezipped the pocket, then did what he always did, washed Kenneth's shirt, shorts, jockstrap, and socks, added fabric softener in a tumbler ball. Returning to his desk, he tried to write, found he couldn't. He called the phone number but hung up. In the drying cycle forty minutes later, he sprinkled a bleaching agent in the lining of Kenneth's jockstrap, undecided if it was out of revenge, jealousy, or heartbreak. It was all three.

NORMAN PUSHED AWAY from his desk with a sudden awareness that he had held his breath through the sheer act of remembrance. Breathless, that was how he would describe it, now and in the years to come. He still longed for a visceral intimacy. So why, then, had he not simply talked to Kenneth, brought the infidelity out into the open? Was the relationship so irrevocably lost? Wasn't it how normal relationships proceeded—through injury and healing, through confession and redemption?

He felt a bewildering sense of pain. Kenneth had awakened the possibility of physical intimacy that had been short-circuited by a closeted adolescent life, though it didn't help that there had been other determinants, events, and memories predating Kenneth. Namely, the bogeyman drama of John Wayne Gacy that came in the first stirring of his own homosexual awareness as he had sat passively, yet secretively attentive to the unfolding horror perpetrated by a clown pedophile businessman who had shaken Rosalynn Carter's hand. Gacy, by all accounts an upstanding citizen, a man who lived in plain sight, groomed a cadre of young adolescents with his magic tricks—his coin behind the ear and handcuffs—luring his victims to his home and basement with the promise of employment, leading them to their eventual strangulation amidst his ejaculatory release, his wife in the kitchen above him.

What had captivated, frightened, and yes, fascinated Norman, was the contained life a person could live, how Gacy lived and murdered in the precincts of his own home. It taught Norman a lesson, how life could be so concealed, compartmentalized, how a sense of one's desires—or, equally, one's ambitions—could be serviced amidst the lives of others. In the associative nightmare of his coming of age, stashing his own gay magazines in, of all places, the crawlspace in his parents' home, he detrimentally came to align himself with Gacy, sexual release associated with the smell of crawlspaces. Norman closed his eyes, tried to block a sense of an old fear, hearing in his head again the internal dialogue he had maintained with his glossies as he entered the emptiness of his house in the absence of his parents. Yes, Norman Price, the original *Latchkey Kid*, descending into the basement, crawling into the literal and figurative hole of his psyche, unburying his glossies, his pants around his ankles, cock in hand, a wad of cum shot in a simultaneous moment of ecstasy and convoluted guilt.

How did a man like Norman Price speak to such sublimated homosexual nightmares that seemed so patently against the homosexual cause in its modern incarnation? How had the celebration of alternative lifestyles been achieved in a matter of decades, so nobody spoke of the time before, of the history of shame and fear that lived, even now, deep within Norman Price? These were the questions that dogged him. In the present openness of his life, in the shared partnership with his lover, Kenneth, in his role as father to a child, he had accomplished things he would never have dreamt possible way back at the beginning of his adolescent awakening. He felt a measure of personal redemption that he had survived a great personal crisis. He had overcome so much.

Any biography should surely have to mention all this. And now it was ruined.

IN THE SURFACING morning light, Norman saved and closed his file for the day, understanding his life would never be the same again. He had the provisional goods on Kenneth's lover, Daniel Einhorn. Einhorn had rowed at Yale. He was older than Norman, but he had the broad shoulders and strong neck of his rowing days. He disquietingly reminded Norman of Mr. Feldman, the assured sense of entitled privilege, not to mention the proximity of Einhorn's home in Winnetka, 1.3 miles from Mr. Feldman's.

Kenneth was supposed to call in five minutes. It was part of a new regularity, part of Kenneth's intimate deceit of sharing two lovers, keeping one partner at bay while hurrying to the gym where Daniel Einhorn was waiting.

Norman was aware that he had been counting off the minutes. He felt his heart race. Six weeks earlier, he had created a facsimile of a Department of Health letterhead and seal and posted a fake form letter to Daniel Einhorn's home address, stating: "Department of Health Code regulations mandate we advise you a recent sexual partner has tested HIV-positive. You are required to alert other sexual partners immediately and seek medical consultation in accordance with Illinois State Medical Statute 1043."

Using the United States mail in such a manner was a felonious act, or was it? He had impersonated a state agency, but he had not sought to extort or defraud. It was difficult determining how the letter might be legally interpreted. Internet searches had come up inconclusive, but in the act of searching the internet, he knew he had furthered a forensic trail. Yet it paled against his not having worn gloves to ensure his fingerprints could not be traced. And he had *licked* the envelope. What sort of dramatist made such fateful mistakes? These were elemental mistakes, but mistakes that spoke to the realities of life, to the inconclusive resolve in matters of the heart—for what else constituted life, really, but matters of the heart?

At the Chicago Union League Club, Norman had a bouquet of black roses waiting for Kenneth, a macabre and effete gesture. They were unsigned. Let him fret! He would let the breakup unfold in the foyer of the club. Let Daniel Einhorn console Kenneth. Let Daniel Einhorn see what it was like to carry the dead weight of Kenneth Birch! Let the breakup play out in the resplendent waspish atmosphere of the Union League. Let Kenneth see what it was like to be dumped. Let him feel that deep pain. Let Kenneth come back begging.

Wasn't that what Norman essentially wanted—a spluttering atonement? What Kenneth needed to learn was how great Norman truly was! There was time yet to reclaim love. What Kenneth needed to do was come crawling back.

NORMAN TURNED TO a story on the early morning news involving an incident from the previous evening's commute—an emergency vehicle's crablike claw extraction of a car from Lake Michigan. A running tickertape listed the victim, Helen Price, as in critical condition. All morning, Norman had been waiting for a call from his father, steeled against sobering first words of atonement, some attempted reconciliation, the unsettling voice of his father revealing where he was and what was happening.

Would he go see his mother? He debated it all morning, setting it as his choice, when it wasn't. His father never called. He had not talked to either of his parents in four years.

What surfaced in the more immediate moment was the smarting pain of Kenneth's infidelity. He needed Kenneth, and yet he had acted contrary to his emotions. Sending black roses to the health club had been a distracted act, offsetting the more immediate crisis of his mother's accident, a pattern of passive aggression that had defined much of his life.

And then the phone rang. Norman answered on the second ring. He half-expected his father's voice. He heard instead the exasperated rush of Kenneth's voice.

"God, what a morning!"

Norman was stilled into silence, and Kenneth, mistaking the silence as recalcitrance made a noise of sudden dissatisfaction. "I was called into work. You get it? I work! You don't own me!"

Norman said flatly, "You're done. Come home. We can all go out to breakfast."

Kenneth's impatience flared. "You heard what I said? You don't own me. You're pathetic, you know that?"

It confirmed for Norman where Kenneth was. He felt a pit in his stomach. He said with a flat insistence, "When did the offer of a free breakfast become pathetic?"

Grace appeared in the hallway. She was talking harshly in Chinese to one of her Barbies. On occasion, Norman had witnessed her put a doll's head into the toilet bowl. He shouted, "Damn it. Stop!"

Kenneth, assuming the remark was directed at him, shouted, "You don't get to speak to me like that, asshole!"

Norman, suddenly aware of the misunderstanding, pleaded, "Wait!"

It was too late. Kenneth was already hung up, gripped by a lust that takes hold in those moments of longing that cannot be appealed to through the faculties of reason or any of the emotions that should bind and hold a person.

He had a date to fuck Daniel Einhorn.

Four

WALTER AWOKE TO a rattle of a cart passing in the hallway. Helen had survived. According to her attending physician, it was a combination of the pills and the freezing water. Both blunted her fight or flight response. Submersion into freezing water triggered a primal diving reflex, shunting blood to vital processes. There were cases of survivors pulled from freezing water who made full recoveries.

Walter whispered Helen's name, said it a second time. There were instances, he had been told, when a patient could hear what was being said but not respond, and sometimes patients miraculously awoke and remembered all that had been said, Walter conscious that if Helen awoke, it would be into the cold reality of finding not just him but Cancer awaiting her return. It made him cold and hard to the facts of life. It would have been better if she had died. It was just a statement of fact.

A CALL CAME just before seven-thirty from a detective. Walter stepped into the hallway. Certain facts were emerging. Eyewitnesses in the last seconds before Helen plunged into the lake had observed an unmarked car behind her turn on its siren, suggesting Helen may have hit the accelerator instead of the brake.

A downloaded image of the car's license plate from a traffic camera identified the car as Walter's. The revelation poured something cold down his spine.

The investigator continued. "Eyewitness accounts say the unmarked car waited until the victim's car entered the water, then abruptly headed north."

There was again, a sudden silence, then the deadening statement, "You have been identified as the driver."

In the voice, Walter understood there would not be the alliance there had once been.

There was a momentary pause. "Pending an investigative review, you are on administrative leave."

The line went dead, Walter understanding his career and life were over.

BY A VENDING AREA, Walter lost fifty cents to a coffee machine that didn't work. When he turned, a nurse was on the phone. She looked away. He understood she was communicating with authorities, that certain measures were underway, the state attorney's office undoubtedly seeking an injunction to bar him from again entering Helen's room.

Walter thought of calling Norman, then realized he had erased the number long ago. He could dial directory assistance, but he didn't. It was too late for reconciliations. Instead, he turned toward the coming day, his breath shallow in his chest. How to assess that moment when it ended? It was there, dammed off, all that had been lost to him and so early. In the fall of 1973, to confirm his suspicions, he had tailed Helen and Mr. Feldman to a National Insurance Convention in Detroit, watched them leave under cover of dark, head east, then north, arriving eventually at the diminished honeymoon gateway of Niagara Falls.

He recalled a solitary vigil outside a motel on the American side, a night passing into morning, Helen appearing into blue skies and headed for a bank. And later, trailing them into the grey mist of the Canadian side, into what turned out to be an assemblage of vintage carnival rides, sideshow attractions, Ripley's Believe It or Not! and Madame Tussauds Wax Museum, a sepia shot of a man going over the falls in a barrel, this what human spectacle had looked like in the nineteenth century, a vaudevillian fascination with Houdini, Tiny Tim, and any number of bearded ladies and alleged mermaids.

Ahead, Walter watched Mr. Feldman and Helen walking side-by-side. It was like a Hitchcock movie, *North by Northwest*, the broad expanse of a continent at their disposal. He had imagined their eventual union, Helen undoing her coat, unbuttoning the flounce of her blouse, unclasping her bra, slipping out of her skirt, rolling down her nylons over each thigh, Mr. Feldman with his arms behind his head on the bed.

It was while he was standing near a sizzle of sparks thrown from a cage of bumper cars that he witnessed Mr. Feldman take an envelope from Helen and approach a figure in a hunter's plaid jacket. It had confused him. Were they venturing further into the northern reaches for some river lodge stocked with bourbon and cigars, a postcolonial hideaway where Mr. Feldman might live out the remainder of his life fly-fishing?

Walter watched the exchange of money. The man in the hat turned, looked toward a girl, heavily pregnant. Mr. Feldman's eyes, and then Walter's, drawn to a native girl. Mr. Feldman made a move to go to the girl, but the man stopped him, Walter seeing, in an instant, the same outline of squared jaw on both men, now aware what he was seeing. The Vietnam War had turned Mr. Feldman's eldest son, Nate Feldman, the draft dodger, into a Thoreau-like figure lost to the Canadian north.

With Nate Feldman's departure, Mr. Feldman reached for Helen's hand. She gave it, Walter aware what was lost and would never be regained.

The nurse said Walter's name and had said it a number of times. He looked up.

She approached in what amounted to a stalling maneuver, a security detail on its way. She offered him coffee. Pinned to her uniform was a large circular button with a portrait of her three children, Walter struck by the declarative sense of how simply a life could be defined and presented to the world.

He said, "You have beautiful children," then pointed his gun at her heart.

WITH THE PILLOW centered over Helen's face, the struggle was immediate. In those final moments he thought of the first dates of their courtship in the pressing days of the Cuban Missile Crisis, lunch hours spent at an automated vending cafeteria, a Jetsons-style vision of the future that broadly missed how the future eventually turned out. They had talked about—or *he* had talked about—Castro and Khrushchev, the missteps of a naïve Kennedy and the disaster of the Bay of Pigs, in a time when history was less generous in its assessment of Kennedy's presidency, their relationship developing against what could have been the last days of the Earth. In truth, he had never known happier times. He remembered, too, the flecked gold in Helen's green eyes, not unlike the speckled Formica countertop, both of them sitting amidst the petrochemical smell of the diner with its cellophane-wrapped entrées, the plastic knives and forks, the Styrofoam cups and plates, the eye-watering hairspray smell of her hairdo, the suffocating acrylic of her nails, all of it of its time, in an age of chemical romance, improvement, and bombs.

In its aftermath, when it was done, Walter put the gun to his open mouth and fired.

PART II

All happy families are alike;
each unhappy family is unhappy in its own way.
—LEO TOLSTOY

Five

NOBODY JUMPED TO their death in the financial meltdown as they had in the crash of 1929, a fact Norman Price wryly observed, the lack of a defining moment, despite the losses equaling or surpassing the crash of '29, so it was not an end in the way the Roaring Twenties had collapsed in the run on banks and chaotic dissolution of so many lives.

Rather, the financial meltdown was a "correction," albeit a serious correction. Complicated explanations emerged—namely, the rise of derivative markets alongside mortgage-backed securities bundled as investment instruments that, enigmatically, nobody could now unbundle, suggesting the financial fallout and its long-term effect was incalculable and would be for the foreseeable future, as if what was being discussed was an assessment of the amount of dark matter in the universe and not simply what it should have been, a forensic accounting of dollars and cents.

There were the lightweights on the network morning shows peddling explanations. Al Roker and the like, weathermen, the uninformed educating the even less informed about the volatility of the securities markets, while a rambunctious plebiscite from places like Biloxi, Mississippi; Billings, Montana; and Cedar Falls, Iowa, pressed into Times Square, held up signs like "We Luv U Al!" and "We Luv the Big Apple!" in their collective force, affirming certain undeniable truths, that, whatever the circumstances, whatever the outcome of the crisis, life would go on.

To Norman Price, it augured the death of history. There would be no revolution, not now or in the foreseeable future, while on the TV he observed how rancor fell inevitably along party lines up on Capitol

Hill—at issue, the Clinton administration's alleged culpability in sponsoring ill-advised subsidized mortgage programs for the poor, which had propagated across the mortgage industry as a whole, facilitating a housing bubble by a loosening of lending practices and no money down, so by the time of the crisis, taxpayer-backed government mortgages accounted for a whopping $10 trillion exposure, a figure representing half the US mortgage inventory.

This was the emerging story—misguided liberal compassion. It played out on the conservative news outlets, a damning indictment of a socialist-minded hubris in a fatal misunderstanding of all-things-financial, the mortgage industry debt tied to behemoth, government-backed programs with names one might have been forgiven for associating with bucolic characters from *The Waltons* or *The Andy Griffith Show*, the doddering genteel sisters, Fannie and Sallie Mae, characters only to be outdone by Freddie Mac, a name suggestive of a would-be affable character from Cosby's *Fat Albert* Saturday morning cartoon, when the mortgage programs, for all their destructive and far-reaching power, might otherwise have been called (and should have been called) "Death Star I" and "Death Star II."

In truth, for anybody who gave a shit, it was difficult deciding what was what and who was at fault. Sometimes too much freedom, too much democracy, too much choice, too much talk could—and did—have the opposite effect, so nothing was achieved, the crisis descending eventually into an argument not over substantive policy but over a defense of free market economics versus socialism, an easy, patriotic dividing line, all the while the underlying reality emerging on both sides of the aisle that the transnational institutions behind the crisis were just "too big to fail."

And so $700 billion materialized in the TARP bailout, as if the money hadn't come from somewhere, upending a fundamental truth, a cast-iron truth tied to lessons learned during the last death throes of the Weimar Republic, where in the run against prudence, in the printing of a useless currency, German citizens wheeled barrows of inflationary money to purchase a pack of cigarettes or loaf of bread on the eve of the rise of Hitler.

Wasn't this how the laws of supply and demand worked in an ever-spiraling hyperinflationary economics of simply printing money, an economic law akin to gravity? He had always been led to believe this, but it was turning out not to be the case, the value of money, its intrinsic worth, decoupled from the gold standard, so there was no underpinning valuation marked against a Fort Knox reserve of tangible gold bullion.

FOR NORMAN PRICE, in the midst of his own crisis, the financial meltdown was a conscious distraction, a postmodern incarnation of indeterminate perpetuity, signifying there were no longer any essential truths, no governing principles, no longer a beginning, middle, or end to events, a state of existence that eclipsed the passing of his parents, thus staving off his need to mourn them—philosophically, what were their deaths in relation to the greater context of what was unfolding? It was all part of a great continuum.

A probate will served as an eventual directive, detailing that Helen had wanted to be cremated. Another will, drawn up by Walter, detailed a similar wish. Norman learned about it in a grim correspondence of legal documents that eventually found their way into his life as he inherited his parents' collective possessions, the house, associated bonds and stocks, along with their ashes.

He called a week after their passing, entered the code to the old-fashioned answering machine, listened to the voice of the secretary from the oncologist's office, asking Helen to confirm her appointment, along with numerous calls from a Mr. Ahmet.

For his own artistic interests, he made a recording of the recording, so the sound and quality was diminished. When he played it back, it sounded like a track deep in Pink Floyd's *The Wall*, the transatlantic trunk call, an operator hanging up, the dropped call, the operator giving up, and the caller left with the disconsolate hurt of what it felt like to call and find nobody home.

IN THE INTERIM since his parents' passing, life had radically changed, Norman venturing out into the cold dark of a Chicago night in early November, holding Grace's hand in throngs pressing down on Grant

Park in the rousing anticipatory sense history was being made. John McCain, distinguished and decorated former prisoner of war, had been unable to overcome the rainbow coalition of minorities and women voters unsettled by the fallout of a post-9/11 response of lies that had led to the wars in Afghanistan and Iraq and contributed to the collapse of the economy.

On the night of Obama's win, Kenneth called from a bar. In the drowning sound of uproarious celebration, his voice was hard to hear. He went out and stood in an alley. He and Norman were separated in a mutually agreed cooling-off period, Kenneth caretaking Daniel Einhorn's downtown apartment, though circumstances were changing, Kenneth candidly revealing how Einhorn's financial dealings were under review by the securities commission. He intimated that Einhorn might yet do time, his assets under threat of seizure.

Norman understood where the conversation was leading, but he offered no advice when he might have broached a reconciliation, asked Kenneth to come home. He didn't. Instead, he listened in the lull of indecision, this all Kenneth's doing. He heard Kenneth's teeth chatter, offered a salve of concern, saying, "You'll catch your death."

Kenneth hesitated. He asked about Grace before tentatively asserting what he felt were his legal rights as parent, Norman laughing at the temerity of a pauperized Kenneth pushing this absurd idea that he had any leverage.

Norman said abruptly, "You made your bed, now lie in it."

Kenneth was abruptly confrontational. "I know about the fake letter you sent Daniel from the Department of Health. He could have your ass in jail!" Kenneth clicked his fingers like Norman's life could be ruined just like that.

It put a fear in Norman that lasted a day, and then another and another, what Kenneth was capable of doing, whereafter, upon further consideration, Norman understood that whatever about Kenneth, Daniel Einhorn was never going to embroil himself in an accusation that would implicate him in a gay affair. This was the sort of discombobulation of rational thought Kenneth could incite in Norman, and in understanding it, Norman doubled down on his understanding that he was better without Kenneth in his life.

In truth, losing Kenneth was a great burden unloaded, a feeling that eclipsed most everything else going on around him, approximating a feeling he was hearing about everywhere, a self-styled austerity measure of personal reform, a feeling of what it was like to cut up your credit cards, attested to by honest folk earnestly giving testimonials on conservative talk radio about assuming personal responsibility in a quasi-religious atonement for wrongful purchases, all of it suggesting that there was nothing fundamentally wrong with America or with the Constitution or with capitalism for that matter. It was just the *people* who had strayed and needed to make amends. Norman had, as people were collectively putting it, just made "bad choices," personal politics obviating the need for true institutional reform. It was up to him to change.

IN THE QUIET of the early morning, Norman turned from his typed notes. In the hall mirror, he watched his now live-in nanny's Weimaraner, Randolph, stir and go toward the bathroom.

This was part of what he was calling "The New Existence." He listened to the faint lapping sound of the dog drinking from the toilet bowl. Randolph then entered Grace's room again. Norman tracked him in the mirror, watched him stretch out before an internment of naked Barbies lined up beside Grace's dollhouse in what looked like an ongoing tribunal of alleged crimes, Randolph a jaded intermediary of an irreconcilable Lilliputian conflict.

Norman had scenes in his head, discreet moments that might be eventually staged. Dogs were exemplary in portraying man's inhumanity to man, man's best friend corrupted. Norman imagined a play, Randolph dressed up in a Nazi storm trooper uniform with perhaps a monocle to give focused malevolence to his face and snout. Each room, a scene in his head.

Joanne Hoffmann, Randolph's owner and now Grace's nanny, was also up, involved in a series of contorted Yogalates holds in his living room, her flannel pajama bottoms riding low on the spread of her pelvis. Norman had hired her at the beginning of the New Year, a neighbor fallen on hard times. Her long-term partner had dumped her. Norman learned the disconsolate details New Year's Eve, at close on nine thirty in the apartment hallway as Joanne had stepped out to walk the dog, revealing, after Norman's polite enquiry as to how she planned to ring in the New Year, that she was planning on being asleep before midnight.

She had mentioned her separation with an oblique apology related to the fights that had apparently raged in the final weeks of her breakup, fights that Norman must undoubtedly have overheard, which he hadn't, but that he had felt obliged to pretend he had to give a gravitas to the implosion of what he learned had been a fifteen-year relationship.

It was revealed in one long sentence, management disinclining to extend her lease, her credit shot. Originally from upstate New York, she was considering returning home for good, but there was a family complication. She stopped abruptly, changing the subject. She had a dresser and an antique table, family heirlooms, on Craigslist, priced to sell. She told Norman all this, Randolph pulling, wanting to do his business. She asked if Norman might be interested. She could show him after the dog was let out.

At midnight they rang in the New Year together, a party, if you could call it a party, a celebration cobbled together, Joanne, in the minutes before the New Year, removing cellophane wrap from a tray of cheeses, crackers, and dips Norman bought in the eleventh hour of the dying year. He dusted off two champagne flutes, opened a bottle of champagne so it was done just in time, the clink of glasses after the ball dropped at Times Square, each counting down the seconds, standing at a distance, watching the television.

Grace slept through it, curled in the tapered hindquarters of Randolph. Norman topped off their glasses so they were filled, emptied, refilled, emptied, and refilled again as he marveled at the ease Grace exhibited in the company of the dog, which led to an account of the dog he once owned, Bruce, and how Norman figured dogs served a purpose in making certain truths all too apparent and obvious, what one had the capacity to do under certain circumstances. Granted, not a conversation for a New Year's early morning, but he said it nonetheless, Joanne understanding that nothing was off limits, not his melancholy or pain or hers either. They toasted to "distilled emptiness and god-honest truth."

Joanne wore no makeup. She went into the world unadorned. Norman liked that about her. He told her so that first night. She cried. They hugged like brother and sister. Norman talked about the trip to China to adopt Grace, falling on the eventual undoing of his relationship with Kenneth. It had not been a good last two years.

And so it happened, at the dawn of a new year, this new presence in his life. Soon after, Joanne became a normalizing force, the metaphorical and literal contortions of her holds in the early hours, so even now, watching her, Norman came to think of her life as a one-act drama played to an empty house. He felt, if he were to stage his own life, he would offset her life in an upstage cone of light amidst a general darkness of his own voice, her actions more than her words suggesting a writhing, indeterminate metamorphosis that would come into momentary light, then darkness, then light again, and finally darkness.

She proved the great distraction he needed. It helped that he had tangentially known her partner, the pedantic Peter Coffey, who, after a dissolute eternity as adjunct faculty gained a tenure-track position at a small community college out West. Toward the end, Coffey was openly cheating with a former student, Joanne describing Coffey as a second-rate poet with doughy flesh from indolent study, and truth be known, a poet with a small penis, but then wasn't that the reason behind most bad poetry? Under the influence of liberally poured wine, she could be truculent. She had a way of scrunching her nose and puckering her lips when she got mad, absentmindedly rimming her glass in a circular motion, her eyes glossing with a deepening hurt. She was holding it together, just barely. In that, they shared a mutual hurt.

Grace figured as a point of compassionate maternal direction for Joanne. She had ideas about motherhood and as nanny assumed corrective measures of more one-on-one time, she, Grace, and Randolph forming a conspiracy of sorts that unburdened Norman, reorienting his relationship with all three. He was benefactor and provider, Joanne granting him what she called "alone time" to write, Joanne administrator of rules, inflexible when necessary, but always kind and loving.

NORMAN LOOKED AT the clock. It was not yet six. Joanne would bring him coffee at six-thirty, her idea of matronly service. He did not object. It divided the early morning, gave him a point of reference. In the quiet indeterminacy, looking between Joanne and the outside world, he turned and pulled up the website for the realty agency contracted to offload the house he had inherited. He had used a lawyer and funds liquidated from his parents' estate to have the house listed, market-values-be-damned. He had not gone out to the house.

There was no malice in Norman's not confiding his dealings with Joanne. He was simply unsure what he wanted, but intent on aggregating his assets, not letting the house fall into disrepair, letting it languish too long on the market.

Pulling up the site, he stared at the low-res feed on the virtual walk-through, a grainy fisheye sweep on the screen. Images wavered and stalled in the hallway. To go any further, to view the home in high-resolution, required an email address. It said so in a pop-up window. In the quiet indecision, another pop-up window provided unsolicited financing options—three- and five-year ARMs, balloons, variable and fixed rates, a flashing banner indicating *Bad Credit Isn't a Problem*, a legacy banner, pre–financial meltdown. There were, presumably, no such loans anymore, though the site had not been updated.

Staring at the jittery feed, inhabiting what had been his former life, Norman was eerily reminded of the first scenes of *The Titanic*, the same walk-through of history, a modern submersible sending back a grey feed from beneath the Atlantic to the aged surviving heroine, the once beautiful Rose Dewitt. That was art's genius, its suggestive power to encapsulate, in the case of *The Titanic*, to apprehend the hubris that had so defined the age—the push across the Atlantic at breakneck speed for the record, the film's essential allure, the foreknowledge that those on board were living the last days of their lives and not knowing it, but everybody watching knowing.

Sometimes the fated sense of a past retold had a greater meaning, connecting to a drama closer to the tragedy of the Greeks, *The Titanic*, the all-time highest grossing film, attesting to the fact that even moderns were more comfortable reliving what they already knew than learning something new. It was essentially the same with bedtime stories, a sense of foreknowledge communed, connecting those watching or listening with a complicit omniscience, affirming certain truths and hopes that justice always prevailed.

Norman felt on this morning, in the act of reengagement, in allowing his mind to wander as it might, to fall upon these loose connections, the inherent stirring of a reenergizing intellect taking over after the loss of Kenneth. He was wandering into a creative and searching space, the unmoored flotsam of events washing up in a scud of the subconscious. He was building from what remained, some raft, something that might sustain and carry him forward, liberate and connect him again to his craft.

He liked the double entendre of the word "craft," how the right words and ideas could float in the natural currents toward understanding, if one let oneself be carried, a process that required not so much strength as patience, to assess and reconfigure life, so one could stare back toward the coastline of the inhabited world, then make for shore once more. He still had things to say in life, memories and observations that meant something, that connected to the greater context of his own life. He would get there slowly.

Norman looked up, life stirring in a compactness of isolated sounds, the opening and closing of a door, the creak of a courtyard gate, footsteps heading into the coming day, Chicago at this hour still decoupled from human agency, so he felt what it was to live at the edge of a day that offered nothing. At times, he felt like a fugitive from life itself.

Norman stared again at the computer screen, suddenly aware his mother no longer existed. She had been incinerated to ash. A reflexive tightness gripped his chest, a register of emotion he was not aware he still possessed.

He pulled up the internet memorial site to affirm she had ever existed. A question mark placeholder showed where her picture should have been uploaded but never was. Not a single person had signed the virtual memorial book. On the site, an American flag wavered like a flag plangently planted on the moon, suggesting the afterlife was somehow an American holding. And yet it somehow fit with a certain understanding that his mother had had of the American experience, its striving greatness and sense of possibility pursued and then abandoned in the lunar grey of a destination reached and then forgotten, so he understood, the journey had been the point and not the landing, not the conquest. That was the story of the moon and so much of everything else in life.

He was suddenly glad now for the internet, for the impersonal expediency of how all matters of life and death could now be so negotiated, the disconnectedness of connectedness. All a real funeral would have revealed was the tacit reality that there had been nobody in his mother's life for a very long time. She had opted for an insignificant departure, a literal dropping off the earth into the depths of the great lake, seeking the fathoms of her own grave, taking with her the argosy of her dreams, the air pocket of her retirement ending in the literal rising of a water line in the cab of her car. It fit her temperament, the self-contained ending, the tight circle of her own thoughts and ideas, her immense capacity to withhold opinions, to stay in the orbit of her own existence.

For a moment, his thoughts settled once more with *The Titanic*, on the sullen passing of life in the cold reaches of the North Atlantic far from shore. He hadn't watched *The Titanic* in a long time. In the falling snow, he thought, why not seal off the outside world for a lost day of tragic remembrance? Why not submit to this quiet reprieve, rerun history in the wavering stills, the opening sequence draped in the raiment of the dirge of Uilleann pipes against the siren's lament of Celine Dion? He was, he felt, a Rose Dewitt of a lesser tragedy, but a tragedy, nonetheless. Maybe he could dive as the submersible did, dredge back a history long sunken. Yes, maybe that was what he would do.

Six

To NATE FELDMAN, Helen Price was always The Other Woman, to the point that he didn't recall her name in a letter sent to him by a law firm out of Chicago. Over three decades had passed since he had dodged the draft and gone into the northern reaches of Canada.

He picked the letter up at a PO box on his weekly excursion to town, a remote eight-mile journey along an old logging road. His bladder ached from the grind of the snow-chained tires. He edged toward the glow of Iroquois Falls, the world encased in a dark that in late January held past 9:30 A.M.

A storm was forecast, his radio tuned to the Canadian weather service, the barometric pressure dropping fast, but he had errands to run. He worked within a window of opportunity. He didn't meet a single car, his eyes focused on the cone of his headlights, old growth pines running sentinel along either side of the road, so at times he felt the last human alive, that he had survived a great cataclysm, which, in a way, he had.

THE TOWN WAS all but deserted, dim yellowing lights aglow in various establishments. He shuffled through the mail in the cold vestibule of the post office. What struck him first was the airmail blue of the envelope. He felt an overwhelming déjà vu, so he had to lean for support against the burnished brass of the PO boxes.

He fingered the waxy envelope, recalling when weight mattered in the economy of early flight, when the envelope was the medium on which one wrote, and when it was done, the folded origami of making it an envelope again, the tongue run along the sweet bordering glue, sealing it. His father had sent him letters to this same PO box with the affectation of *par avion*, letters asking after his health, but more point-edly after Nate's wife and newborn child, though their names were never mentioned under the presumed understanding the letters would be opened by the United States government.

In his pickup, the vents poured a dry heat over Nate's hands. He was overcome with the trailing sentiments of his father's old letters, and his own, written so long ago, under the influence of unearned freedom, knowing others were dying and that he had chosen not to serve. He ran his thumb along the crinkled give of the envelope. He recalled the first summer of his escape against an encroaching wildfire, the sky a blood orange, the thunderous stampede of wildlife in a pitiless retreat toward rivers in a natural divide of a fire line, and then the soot and ash, the tor-rents of rain that darkened the midsummer as though it had all been de-livered unto him alone. He had endured those first months with a moral indecisiveness, so it had been hard to find the measure of who he was.

NATE DIDN'T OPEN the letter right away, holding off past the insistent pressure of youth. He exited the pickup under a bowl of a streetlight. The wind took the door. He pushed it shut with both hands. A dusting of snow blew around his face. Storm in the air.

In the warm store, he picked up his supplies: coffee, evaporated milk, an assortment of meats, three bags of flour, rice, beans, a kilo of sugar, an allotment of canned goods. He had emailed his order ahead. The goods were sitting in a crate with his name stapled to the slatted wood. He checked the contents against his list. The proprietor, Pierre Arouet, emerged from the domestic quarters. He simply nodded without com-ment, then turned again.

Nate used a bathroom off to the side of the store. He went in dribs and drabs. Blood clouded the bowl. He should see a doctor but knew he wouldn't.

On the road outside of town, Nate looked again at the letter, set be-side him like a passenger come a long way. Ahead, snow fell in a soft swirl that took on the blue grey of a contusion, the north-facing hills cast in cavernous shadow, the western sides a pale butter yellow that had long since sent animals toward the instinctive drowse of hibernation.

He felt the same drugged effect in the shunt of blood toward vital organs. His hands and feet were always cold, in a way they had not been years before. He yawned into the back of his hand.

NATE OPENED the letter at the kitchen table. It referenced some film reels, recordings that had belonged to his father and passed into the possession of Helen Price, who had subsequently bequeathed them to Nate. In view of the reels' age and fragility, the law office was seeking advice on how to proceed.

Nate looked into the gauze of falling snow, the world gone flat and two-dimensional, the letter still in his hand. Then he read it again.

Nothing indicated the content of the reels or how many there were or what they might contain. Were they a series of confessions or admissions, an attempted explanation? Or did the reels simply contain the mundane stuff of accumulated footage connected to the early mania of the handheld camera, his father, preening in advance of appearing on camera, raising his hand as he walked in and out of the frame in a series of outtakes? It was difficult deciding their significance. But what could not be discounted was that the reels had been kept all these years and bequeathed, not through the execution of his father's will but through his father's apparent mistress, Helen Price. It suggested a lingering, kept secret.

In his small bedroom, Nate retrieved a sweater in a cedar chest he had built with his own hands, the wood giving off a piney tang. The smell dropped to the depths of his soul, the shavings curled amidst folded wool sweaters, socks, and hats. He had become fastidious in his solitude, in the quiet arrangement of everything in its rightful place. He stood in the room, everything waiting to take on the approximation of existence.

AT A SMALL DESK, Nate turned on his computer. He found a reference to Helen Price's accident and articles related to a gruesome murder-suicide. At the end of her obituary was mention of a surviving son, Norman Price, an established Chicago playwright.

In his kitchen, Nate opened a can of soup, set it on the stove. A crowning flame licked the gloom. An argument proceeded within him.

He was content here. He had cords of wood stacked, a root cellar filled with potatoes, rutabaga, beets, and wild onions, along with dried berries and walnuts, canned apples and jars of honey, all gathered throughout a summer of endless light. He had proved capable with an axe, acquired a knack for survival when others might not have fared as well. He considered this a great personal realignment with the natural order of the universe.

Nate stared at the letter as he ate. He could ignore it or simply write and refuse delivery. He could instruct that the film reels be destroyed. It was his prerogative.

He muttered a catalogue of excuses for why not to respond. It mattered little what his father might now say. Their correspondence had declined in the protracted later stages of the war, until his father had stopped writing, and Nate, in deference, had quietly and dutifully receded. A congressional act was later passed, dropping charges against those who had dodged the draft. Nate had been free to return to America, but he hadn't.

Seven

S IX WEEKS HAD PASSED in what Norman was calling "The New Existence," which dovetailed with his quietly anointing Joanne "The Refugee of Suburbia" as he watched her set up a dramatic encampment of a makeshift tent of sheets draped over the heirloom antique table out in the living room.

Joanne had promised the table would be gone in no time. It wasn't. Confoundedly, it was still on Craigslist, when it was, in her words, "a real steal." Norman wasn't an economist, but he liked the idea of working with logic problems, and under the terms of "The New Existence" he took an active interest in the table as part of an experiment in understanding the essential principles of how life was actually lived—the rise and dash of expectations, rational or irrational, founded or unfounded. These expectations figured in how markets worked, this essential flux of expectation and return on investment.

He had a formula with x, in this case, the heirloom table signified as x, whose value was based on two factors, the table's *perceived valuation (pv)*, what x was allegedly worth, and then what someone eventually paid for x, the *purchase price (pp)*. As he denoted it mathematically in most cases, $pv \neq pp$. He had the table drawn on a white board with intersecting lines connected between various formulations where the table (x) could work out as $pv \neq pp$, $pv < pp$, $pv > pp$, or, in this current instance, where there was no transaction at all. He denoted this as $pv \otimes pp$. These formularies were connected to what Norman was dubbing an individual's Happiness Quotient (*hq*), something akin to Maslow's Hierarchy of Needs. It proved a great distraction, the whiteboard formulas accounting for all manner of social and economic interactions.

In the background, Norman kept a small TV on C-SPAN for the

belief that this was how democracy worked, that people of sound principle were working on correcting markets and realigning freedoms, the chambers of both houses emptied and then filled in the rolling noise of seats being taken, sworn testimony given and accounted for.

This was all part of "The New Existence"—reform, self-analysis, accountability, and transparency—the great show of collective reconciliation. He thought it crap but gave himself to the moment. History had its own undertow of persuading influences. What he cynically submitted to was the spectacle.

The hearings captivated Joanne. She had the TV on in the living room. She liked the crisp cleanness of congressional and senatorial members and their staff, the polite decorum of it all. She was genuinely interested in the power of talk. She had a habit of setting her hands on her hips, listening. The extent of the losses was astounding. She quoted figures. She was, she told Norman in all sincerity, for law and order. She wondered if the Lehman Brothers would eventually testify, then made a face when Norman said nothing. *Hello*! She knew the Lehman Brothers were dead! She made a face at Norman.

She took liberties in casually interrupting him. He didn't altogether mind. She wanted his opinion as to whether a certain senator wore boxers or not. She liked sincerity in a man more than anything else. She looked between the TV and Norman, Randolph following her gaze.

What Joanne was teaching Norman, what he observed sitting in his office, turning to stare into the reflected image of the hallway mirror, was the small revelatory accumulation of acts and details. Joanne's ease and attentiveness in dressing Grace in matched socks and color-coordinated outfits, or his coming upon them in the kitchen, Joanne cutting food into bite-sized bits and requiring that all steamed broccoli, cauliflower, sprouts, and spinach be eaten before there was even mention of dessert, standing over Grace in a détente that sometimes lasted a half hour, Grace marched to her room to think about "making better choices," when Norman would have simply given in, not out of love, but expediency.

At times, he wanted to put Joanne on the spot, ask about *her* apparent bad choices (*bc*), and yet he learned to quell his natural cynicism. Through the act of talking in an associative pantomime of actions expressed through language and body, a child eventually navigated the world. This was how you shored up the silence of a day, how language and idiom were conveyed in the banter of describing an action. He wrote it all down in its exacting details, revising and coming up with additions to his new formulary of life's grand equation.

There were a series of equations that constituted the day. Joanne requested that Grace be fitted out with a new coat and boots for their meandering lake walks with Randolph. Since the purchase, there was the added equation—Joanne and Grace's prewalk routine—Grace demanding that she be allowed to wear Princess Aurora underwear or Belle underwear, so the formula was skewed by a tantrum (t). A tantrum (t) could rise exponentially, denoted by tx. He formulated it. The tantrums and the sociopolitical reality beneath them: the polyester prints purchased at Walmart that shot his stand against globalization and child labor exploitation to hell. This, he rationalized, was economic life under "The New Existence," where princess print underwear could be bought for the price of a Big Mac, and how this inextricably connected to why there was no middle class anymore—whereas, at one point, with fewer options, people had been committed to saving for a home, banks then demanding a 20 percent down payment, this before homeownership was turned into a casino of no-money-down.

It was a formulation of the children (c), the parents (p), choice (ch), and the banks (b), an interconnected series of events, a mathematical formulation of the butterfly effect.

He had his working formulas, seeking what he was calling the elusive dark matter of the human condition. He felt at the far reaches of a deep and profound understanding of a multiverse view of existence where there might be no single solution, where each case was the exception, a concept that had at its center a spiritual and transcendent dimension. He was slowly getting there.

NORMAN WAS AGAIN staring at the wavering walk-through of his old home on the realty site when Joanne emerged, suddenly standing before him. She held out a cup of coffee and asked, "What are you working on?"

Norman answered with a feigned, albeit determined seriousness, turning from the screen, tacitly blocking it. "A grand theory of relativity that will account for everything we have ever felt or experienced."

Joanne asked, "And it's coming along well?"

"Not really . . ."

Joanne shrugged, "Well, there's always tomorrow, right?"

Norman conceded, "Yes, tomorrow . . ."

It was then that Joanne saw the wavering feed of the realty site. Her eyes shifted from the site to Norman. It was obvious that he had been trying to hide it.

He said preemptively, turning to the screen in a full disclosure, "It's a house I inherited," qualifying the remark, "My parents' house. In the suburbs."

Joanne tried to say something but couldn't, then she gathered herself. Her voice was direct, "If you have plans, I'd like notice, ok?" Looking toward the whiteboard, despite her best efforts, her eyes teared, the détente of their shared existence so suddenly undone.

Norman ventured to explain, but Joanne spoke over him. "Don't!" She raised her hand. "Just don't."

She left the room, then turned around and returned. She said, "Can I be honest with you?" A moment passed. "It's about your work . . ."

Norman felt a chill run through him.

"Peter and I . . . we went to one of your shows, *Latchkey Kid* . . . And you know what I thought about the show? I thought it lacked humanity . . ."

Norman tried to breathe without actively being seen to do so.

Joanne's eyes widened in admitting it. She continued. "Peter, he defended you. He said you were . . . I don't know . . . something Peter would say, *'reappropriating darkness . . .'*"

Norman tried to recover and half laughing, said, "You're making me like Peter."

Joanne nodded. "I bet *you* would! Peter was always generous in describing the failure of others. He said there was genius in facing a darkness too few tried to confront anymore. Of course, he was talking about his own work as much as yours. And you know what I said when he was finished? I said, 'That might be all well and good, Norman Price might be all those things, but he's also an asshole.'"

In the sudden vacuum, Randolph came forward in a slow gait, Joanne confronting the sullen awareness that, in speaking, she had disrupted the balance of not just Norman's life but her own. Her eyes teared again, but not before she said, "I should take him out before he shits. I wouldn't want you to kill him!"

In the suddenness of their absence, Norman waited, listening as Joanne descended the stairs. He was standing outside Grace's room, the door ajar, Grace still asleep.

He took a deep breath. Joanne had touched a nerve, the stinging accusation that his work lacked humanity registering as an unflattering but damning truth. His misanthropy was everywhere, graphed on the whiteboard, in equations of how much time was taken from his interests, as though life could be so compartmentalized.

Staring at Grace, he understood that he been rash in adopting her, that he had done it for his own sense of unbridled liberal views and less with a real understanding of what parenting meant. When he thought about her future, when he tried, and he had, there was an emptiness, a feeling that emerged in those awful plays that went nowhere, ideas and plot lines that were never made quite real, failures, not for a lack of will, but in an inability to sustain the mundane, the ordinary, to buoy existence in the infinite possibility of what a minute, an hour, or a day might hold, and then align it with a guiding foreknowledge of where it might lead and eventually end.

Norman surveyed Grace's room, his eyes drawn to her dollhouse and to the porcelain figurines within—the miniature proprietor, George Crumby, respectable banker, enjoying an eternal breakfast with wife, Esther; son, Harold; and daughter, Polly, a proper Victorian family. It was easy to conjure a life inside the dollhouse, this world fashioned and conceived in a time before two world wars and the collapse of the British Empire, in a time before the leaching of civility, good manners, and proper dress. He had the relevant history, the facts, the apparent mood of crusty manners, the staid voice of George Crumby, speaking over the rasp of a knife spreading butter on toast, speaking with a measure of rebuke, reprimand, or instruction. Though what was more difficult to articulate was the in-between time of the great mansions, what came after George Crumby and his family, the subtle changes when a time was no longer as it was.

WHEN JOANNE came through the door, she headed toward the coat closet, her voice purposefully direct and unemotional. "I can give a month's notice. We never agreed to formal terms, but I think it fair!"

Norman let her finish, then said, "I just checked. There's no law against practicing literary criticism without a license."

Joanne's back was still turned. She stiffened and said, "Whatever you think about me, that board is not my *goddamn* life!"

Norman said, "I'm sorry."

In replying, Joanne turned and faced him. "So am I."

Norman said quietly, "I'd like you to stay. I was wrong. I admit it."

Joanne didn't answer immediately. She looked directly at Norman. "*If* I stay, and I don't know if I will, I'm doing it for Grace, got it?"

The "got it" suggested a turn of mood and tone, a reorienting toward smoother waters, though Norman was compliantly contrite.

Joanne added, "And I want a written contract!"

Norman nodded. "You write one up and I'll sign it."

It ended or seemed to. Joanne offered, "I'm open to making coffee?"

Norman said, "I'd like that."

He went back into his office. He considered closing the site but didn't in the full disclosure of this new agreement.

Joanne returned with a pot of coffee and a mug. As she poured, she said in a conciliatory way, "For the record, what you do . . . it's important . . . I was speaking out of hurt."

Norman said forthrightly in responding, "For every honest line, there are so many others where what is said is not quite right . . ."

The sentiment was lost on her. She said something inaudible, hesitated, then said, "It's just that I've been here three months, and you know what hurts . . . you've never asked me about me . . . not once, not after New Year's."

Norman answered, "I didn't think I had a right to pry."

"Well, pry, damn it! Okay?"

Norman said, "Okay."

Joanne nodded like an arrangement had been agreed to, but it was clear that she was unsettled. She said, "I've a confession to make . . . I looked up Peter last week. That constitutes a betrayal, right?"

Norman knew better than to answer.

"The college where he works is like nothing that he would have ever dreamt of settling for in a million years." Joanne trailed off, shaking her head. "You're busy . . ."

Norman raised his voice. "I'm listening. . . . I'm always after new material." It was a remark that could have been misconstrued, but Joanne advanced on what she needed to say. "Okay . . . for material," putting stress on the word "material."

"When I first met Peter, he had this dream of a New England college where he'd teach and write poetry. He was finishing his dissertation. He had prospects, or I thought so. I was on the rebound. I met him writing at a café, cliché, right? He caught me staring at him. It gave him the upper hand. He referred to it when things fell apart, but for a time, he was good for me. We spent long nights at the library. I'd run errands, get books. He interviewed that spring. We awaited offers. He felt sure of a certain college's interest. They loved his work, that's what he told me. We planned accordingly. And yet no offer came, not from that college or any other. He taught adjunct, padded his resume. It was what was needed, more experience. It was how it went. You served your time in the trenches. That's how he described it. Another round of interviews came and passed. There was nothing he did wrong, not that I could see. I was his biggest advocate. There were just too many candidates. I believed it. He began seeing a student at the night school where he taught. I made excuses for him. I waited. I even bought the same perfume his mistress wore. Crazy, right? I was too caring, too considerate . . . too desperate. Then I got a call about my father."

Norman advanced on the story, asking, "A call. . . ?"

Joanne nodded. "On New Year's Eve, I told you I could never go home, but I never told you *why*! It's on account of my sister, Sheryl."

Norman repeated the name, aware this was a locus of great hurt.

"Dad had worked a union job all his life, swing shift, and to Dad, Sheryl represented hope. . . . She had all As. Everything he did, he did with Sheryl in mind. He wanted a better life for her, then, junior year, she fell for Dave Bishop, who was in his midtwenties. He had barely graduated high school, had a kid already, and was waiting on union work, or that's what he told Sheryl when back then they were handing out pink slips. A union job wasn't what it had once been. Dad swore he'd have a heart attack. There were no union jobs! Dad shouted it. He called Dave a loser. He wouldn't let him near the house. He forbade Sheryl's seeing him. Sheryl accused Dad of self-hate. It went like that. They had been so close, but Dad put his foot down. He was doing it for her own good. He kept saying it. He grounded her. Nothing but school and home. He said that to Mom like she was a jailer. Sheryl's meals were left at her bedroom door. She refused to eat. It went like that. Dad would come home, and first thing he did was go up to Sheryl's room and ask quietly if she'd had a change of heart. He'd lean into the door, waiting. And then one evening, Dad came home at six in the morning, exhausted. He pulled into the drive and Sheryl was there in the kitchen with a pot of coffee. She was dressed in pink robe and slippers. They didn't speak. Sheryl poured. Dad unrolled the morning paper, pretended like there was nothing to be said, and then Sheryl broke down. She said that all she had ever wanted was a man just like Dad. It was the first time I ever heard Dad cry.

"Dave and Sheryl were married her first week out of high school, Sheryl pregnant. They got an apartment. Dave was hired at nonunion wages, let go, and hired back, then let go again. Dad tried to vouch for him. There was just no work. Dave signed up for the National Guard. Two years on, my senior year, they were moved into our garage. I was dating a guy that summer back from Loyola. I left with him. The relationship lasted less than a semester, but there was no going home. Sheryl and Dave had another kid on the way."

Joanne looked at Norman. "Any of this make you think less of me?"

Norman said, "We'll have to consider changing the names to protect the innocent."

Joanne took it as statement of genuine interest. She continued.

"Fast forward a decade. It was near Thanksgiving when I got the call about Dad. Peter knew about Sheryl and Dave. He hadn't earned more than $18,000 a year, and yet somehow Dave and Sheryl made him feel more assured about his past choices. I knew how condescending he could be. We went.

"When we arrived, Dave looked up from fixing a car in the garage. He didn't greet us. It was obvious we weren't welcome. Over the pre-Thanksgiving meal wait, Dave showered and arrived at the house smelling of Brut, the aftershave Dad always wore. I figured it was Dad's. I spent my time trying to talk with Dad. He didn't recognize me, then did, then didn't. He was dressed in a Bills' sweater. I could feel Dave following me with his eyes.

"The kids wanted root beer floats. I went out to the garage to get sodas and ice cream. Dave followed. He had stolen everything from Dad. He spoke to me directly for the first time. He said, 'What are you doing with that fruitcake?' He blocked the doorway. He said, 'You're not half the sister Sheryl is. You left while she stayed.' Then he handed me a card. I couldn't do anything but take it. It turned out that Dave was a member of Promise Keepers, a fraternity of men committed to one woman and one God. It said so on the card, including a list of values and commitments he was sworn to uphold. I didn't know what to say.

"Back in the house, Dave and Sheryl's eldest, Misty, was giving a gymnastics performance. She had been to the Junior Olympics, but she was fighting the natural growth of her figure. Sheryl came into the living room. Dave took her hand. He had his eyes defiantly on me the entire time. When we got home, Peter called me worthless. He was open in his affair. I looked into the Peace Corps, but you know, it's not easy to give yourself up to the prospect of cholera or typhoid or malaria. I was rejected. That Christmas, I got a Christmas portrait card from Sheryl. Dave was holding Misty like Károlyi did that little girl who won the gold medal. Misty had broken her femur. It was what the Lord had ordained, or that's what Sheryl wrote. Dave had all of Misty's trophies piled behind her, like the spoils of Tutankhamen's tomb.

"In the spring, Dad had a stroke. He lasted a week. I went alone to the funeral. Dad had willed the house to Sheryl and Dave. There was nothing in savings. Mom was drawing Medicaid, paying to stay in her own home. I asked Sheryl about a loan. All she did was go stand by Dave. I got nothing. I didn't go to the reception. I just drove away from the grave."

Joanne stopped and said, "A piss poor excuse for my own failings . . . right?"

Norman said, "Sometimes there are no winners and it's all a wash," mindful that anything said was enough, and at times, nothing was demanded save the presence of another.

In the discharge of an emotion spent, Joanne offered, "I could make eggs and toast if you're hungry?" On cue, Grace came forward. She had been standing there listening. She had wet herself in an insistence of recurring nightmares.

Norman rose, and in lifting her, so ended the normalization of what a writing day might have constituted. Along the hallway, he passed Randolph drinking from the toilet, the apartment suddenly a home in way it had not been before.

Eight

THE LETTER was weeks old and curled at the edges. Nate had ignored it like an unwelcome guest, but he felt a question was being asked of him.

Nineteen seventy-one—his arrival into Canada. Thank God for the Canadian wilderness and an undefended border. In the weeks before he left, he had torn pages from an encyclopedia in the public library, circled towns. Havre-Saint-Roche caught his interest, a ramshackle town, historically beset by debauchery and gambling, a town where civilization had never quite taken hold. Most who arrived were felled by malaria, some survived, while others walked into the wilds and were never seen again.

Nate arrived in Havre-Saint-Roche following a night and a day hitching north after crossing the border near the shoals of Sault Ste. Marie, and in so doing affirmed certain truths about life, how hope and progress could sputter and die without ceremony. He was seeking examples of a truncated, lost history, seeking evidence of human insignificance.

Havre-Saint-Roche wasn't really a town anymore by 1971, but a weigh station surviving on a post office and a natural resources station. Nate stayed in the vicinity a week, pitched a small canvas tent along a river's edge, set fishing lines in a pool of still water, until he caught three speckled trout, which he gutted, salted, and added to his supplies. He started a small fire, then wandered amidst the remnants of a rigging, where teams of horses and men had toiled under a boil of black flies and mosquitoes, felling logs that were dragged through a marsh toward a rush of a fast-flowing river.

Nothing had survived intact. He stood in the dappled light between two collapsed dormitories, blue sky shining on a series of identical cots, suggesting the compact sameness of early settlement. In the yawn of a stable door, he looked at the crucible of what had once been a firepit that burned in the service of shoeing horses, making sleds, chains, and irons, along with all manner of tools required for extracting old growth timber, in the center, an accordion bellows like the folded wing of a monstrous bat.

He had not been seeking to restart life but sit out the rush of destruction in the conscientious objection that too much life was discarded by generals in the vainglory of conflicts that might have been resolved if young men refused to serve, if they laid down their arms on both sides, if they chose to run away.

In pages torn from the encyclopedia, he had circled a reference to one particularly ill-conceived mining operation. Financed out of Ottawa, it had sprung up in the dying days of wood, as steel began to be used to rebuild the metropolises along the Great Lakes after the fires of Chicago and Toronto. He found the entrance to the mine, a grim, black mouth agape in the agony of collapse, a splinter of blackened beams within. Twenty-two miners were buried alive a half mile into the side of a hill in a flash flood in the spring of 1929, the calamity meriting just a footnote in the encyclopedia. It proved a prophetic ending Nate needed when he first arrived, inhabiting the cleaving sense of how time could and did outrun the ingenuity of the best-laid plans. *Oh, Canada.*

HE LEFT HAVRE-SAINT-ROCHE in the light of early morning, extinguished his fire with the stomp of his boot, made his way along a dirt road. Grandshire was his destination, a town built by an enlightened industrialist, Augustus Grandshire, a prominent New Englander with progressive sensibilities who transported his vision of a Utopian collective across the border into the wild Canadian backwoods.

The town emerged from a break into a clearing of land run along a river's edge, surviving in its shabby grandeur amidst an overgrowth of tangled foliage. In accordance with its founder's Utopian reach, a pulp mill was set at a distance from the residential district, so Grandshire achieved, at the time, a rarefied divide—separating the toil of one's daily labor from the reprieve of nature. In the town center stood a chapel. At a point, prayer services had been read from a belfry over a loudspeaker, so when the wind blew, people forty miles away claimed to have heard the word of God through the whispering pines.

Nate lodged for two months at what had been a plush hotel, complete with a grand tearoom, velvet-covered couches, and a dance hall with draped curtains.

Everyone understood what brought an American up there, and yet he was regarded with neither suspicion nor interest. Vietnam was not Canada's war. The whirling bite of a blade could cut a man in two. Nate was hired, worked a year that shaped him into a man.

He met Ursula Abenakis soon after he arrived. She was a twenty-two-year-old half-blood native who worked at the hotel. She met his stare with the greenest of eyes, her sallow skin framed by a black sheen of hair. She wrote his name into a leather-bound ledger, the languid sweep of her writing style suggesting a convent education. She had, in fact, been brought up in a Catholicism that never took hold. In the pulse of nature, in daily life, there was a more powerful God.

He took his meals in the hotel dining room, tipping with a view to catching her attention. He watched her fill salt and pepper shakers, top up the milk jugs, turn over the damp brown sugar in the glass bowls, and at the day's end dutifully change the fly-paper strips. He learned, sitting by her in the dying evenings, that her father had been a fur trapper, three-quarters First Nation and a quarter French Canadian, as were most trappers in the region after centuries of interbreeding along fur-trade routes.

Nate was fresh-faced, a young man destined for great things. Or so Ursula told him. It didn't take her long to come out to the cabin he found in the fall, her housewarming gift a rhubarb pie and a pound of ground coffee beans.

At the hotel, she called him "My American," smiling with a beatific grace. He thought her a beauty he could never possess and carried the thought of her in the way men carried lost dreams into battle. He loved her for her intelligence and mystery. When she poured him coffee, he felt like weeping, thinking that he would never have her.

When she arrived with the rhubarb pie, she wore nylons under her jeans, but no underwear or bra. She removed her top without the slightest sense of urgency or impropriety. She observed a polite restraint in the wake of their lovemaking, which was full of struggle and passion. She never asked about his family or if he might return to America.

For her part, she revealed she was from the Anishinaabeg tribe, a name that literally meant, "Beings made out of nothing," a conjuring that set Nate into a swooning sense that, yes, all came from nothing, that all things had to be envisioned and decided upon and then made real. He considered their relationship the same way, something made out of nothing.

Ursula came with a past, something before the current nothingness. She had been with a First Nation man, Frank Grey Eyes, born into the Wolf Clan. They had ventured to Toronto in 1968 so Frank could work construction, but Frank couldn't handle the booze or the loneliness, and though he complained that Toronto was killing him, he stayed and got attached to white women in bars, falling prey to women on the way down. It just exacerbated the decline because it felt like something other than what it was, when it was nothing but the end.

She described how, when Frank was sad, he used to trace the outline of a circle around himself, shuffling in a circular, tribal, tomahawk-wielding dance, a slow vortex spun against the spin of the cosmos, as though he could create some concept of home. He wore his bowler hat, so it was sobering, sad, and moving to witness him dance in the dark of the apartment. Sometimes he scratched a lottery ticket, the silver filings sifting through the air like a spell. He was looking for small, contained miracles. He was fascinated, too, by fortune cookies. He felt revelation hiding in the most unlikely places, and that you had to work against the petulance of the spirit world. Toronto seemed like a place that the spirit world might inhabit. It was worth a look.

Frank was good at understanding the ways of the spirit world. But white women destroyed him. They didn't understand his energy. They could reach in and tear his heart out. There was no magic against white women. Frank was helpless. They passed right through the circle. The last time Ursula saw Frank, he was in a drunk tank. He called her not by Ursula but by a native name that, translated, meant "Something Good Cooking by a Fire." He was bestowing a grace on her, releasing her. His face and nose were smashed in. He kept drawing an invisible circle around himself, so the cops thought he was nuts. Ursula drew a circle around herself and then she was gone. She took a bus back home in the magic of her aura, and so ended the summative history of what had been almost three years of her life. Frank was eventually stabbed to death in Toronto.

Ursula revealed the story, starting a fire Nate couldn't. There was a trick. The embers had to be packed with sawdust dipped in paraffin, which, when lit, gave off a light like the star of first creation, Nate taken by a glint caught in Ursula's eyes, the light licking the sheen of her cleavage and up under her chin as she turned to face him.

BY SEVEN THIRTY, Nate eased toward Windsor. Almost thirty-eight years had passed since his crossing.

He considered calling his only daughter, Aiyana. They had not talked in a great while. Against his and her mother's wishes, she had married a Pakistani immigrant, Rahim Hafeez, who had gone on to great success with a controlling interest in a call center in Karachi. Having inherited English as a native tongue, Rahim's view of English imperialism was exceedingly gracious, though, disconcertingly, he made Aiyana dress according to a conservative Muslim code, while he dressed like any one of the hijackers who had crashed the planes into the Twin Towers—in button-down shirts, Levi's, Nikes, and a Blue Jay's baseball cap.

It was, he understood, an encounter best put off. Perhaps on his return north, he would call.

What figured in his mind was Ursula. Dead eight years, her radiant face was still the trademark design of an organics enterprise that they had started together. He had sketched her face up by Handsome Lake in the first year of their marriage. Under her instruction, she had taught him how to tap maple trees, gather syrup, and later, in the disaster of the onset of an early winter that froze a grape thicket, how to make an ice wine that they ate with a smoked salmon. These items—the maple syrup, the ice wine, the smoked salmon—became synonymous with a rugged Canadian mystique. They added honey and unleavened bread to what became a fledgling gift basket business.

In the ensuing years, he hadn't gone out of his way to tell those who didn't know the origin of the company logo, when it might have increased the sale price of the business. Nor had he revealed his own personal story, his Vietnam history and exile, which might have equally lowered the price. Over time, he had simply changed. His voice leveled with a broadening of his vowels, so he sounded Canadian without consciously trying.

He felt the sudden weight of history, the accumulated years, a life. He sold the company a year after Ursula succumbed to cancer. She would not let him before, insisting he would survive and continue. While she spoke, she gripped his hand. Death meant a crossing, not an ending. She pointed to the trees, to the land, to the animals; she was there in it. He listened to her as he had done all his life, and then she was gone. It was a life he would have lived a thousand times, the most perfect life. His eyes were filled with tears.

NATE HAD his Canadian passport at the ready, his history as an American erased. Approaching the crossing, he could see how the divide between America and Canada had diminished in the push of global sameness, the Eastern Canadian cities along the border filled with the same big box stores, the Walmarts, Lowes, Sears, and Targets; the same fast food franchises, McDonalds and Burger Kings; the same car manufacturers, the GMs and Fords; these Canadian cities now inhabiting just a slightly altered version of the American experience, a reprise of the American experiment overlaid with a sense of decency and socialist tendencies, though it was all becoming a oneness, so there was no real understanding of a divergent past, or it didn't much matter anymore.

Nine

DANIEL EINHORN'S business and personal correspondence was seized in a growing investigation concerning his involvement in a Ponzi scheme. Norman learned it during a phone call with an investigator who asked if Norman knew Daniel Einhorn. Norman said he didn't, then qualifying the remark, saying that though he didn't know Einhorn, they had a mutual friend in common. He didn't say who.

The investigator asked, "Kenneth Birch?" Norman admitted that yes, it was.

Among the documents recovered from Einhorn's office was a faked state health department letter. When asked about its origin, Norman offered no theory but then offered, without referencing the letter, that at one time, he had been in a relationship with Kenneth Birch. It advanced an admission of a relationship gone bad, affirming that the letter was unconnected with the Ponzi investigation, that there was no extortion here, no blackmail, just a jilted vengefulness. The call ended, the investigator offering a perfunctory appreciation of Norman's cooperation.

For Norman it ended a nagging anxiety, his involvement settled in this offhand manner, in the closing of a lead. The Einhorn Ponzi investigation was then capturing headlines, Einhorn's father-in-law the mastermind, the extent of the fraud tapping the zeitgeist of what was part of the unraveling of a failure of governmental oversight under lax deregulatory measures dating to the Reagan years.

A day later, Norman did call Kenneth, seeking tacit corroboration that if pressed, Kenneth would describe Norman's intent in sending the letter as done out of hurt. Norman's prints were on the letter. He was simply covering all bases. Of course, he hadn't planned on saying anything over the phone. They might meet for coffee.

The first call went to voicemail. He tried over a number of days, and in Kenneth's not picking up, Norman understood that Kenneth Birch was truly gone from his life.

AT JOANNE'S INSISTENCE they were going to meet Norman's realtor and do a walk-through of the home, which wasn't moving. Joanne moved in a clip-clop of her heels on hardwood flooring on her way to the bathroom. She left Norman to manage Randolph, who barked at Norman's approach.

Norman stood in the hallway. Joanne was clasping the front tie on a pushup bra, so her cleavage rose and showed. She hadn't been out in the real world in a long time, well, not in the company of a man. She made a pout, applying lipstick. She saw Norman staring and said in an exasperated way, "We're running late. Put Randolph in his cage!"

Norman tried again. Randolph had his own opinions.

Grace emerged. She shouted something in Chinese. Randolph turned. She was holding a naked Barbie doll in one hand as she lured Randolph toward his cage. It did the trick, Grace talking to Randolph, then earnestly to the doll, the way a general might speak to his troops on the eve of some futile battle. Randolph entered the cage, the quarry of the Barbie between his slobbering jowls.

NORMAN'S LICENSE was expired. It had escaped his attention until they were downtown before a Hertz agent. Joanne had a license, but embarrassingly, her credit cards were maxed out. She set them down, one at a time, like a bad poker hand.

On the fourth card, the assistant manager gathered the cards and made a phone call. Two of the cards were in Peter's name, and per company policy, for security purposes, the two were being held. For a moment, it seemed the police were on their way. Hertz was out.

They went with Alamo Rent a Car, a down-market affair along the el track. Norman had to first pay down one of Joanne's cards at his bank since, as sole driver, the rental had to be on a card in her name. All told, it cost him $5,645 to pay off her maxed-out credit card. They settled on a full-size at a teaser rate of $399 for the week, then discovered that Joanne couldn't decline the supplemental coverage at $29.99 a day since she had no car insurance.

THEY LEFT THE SHADOWS of downtown for the shimmer of Lake Michigan and the northern suburbs. Joanne drove close to the barrier along Lake Shore Drive. She passed the intersection where Helen had driven into the lake.

Norman let it pass without comment, though a sullen awareness registered in the finality of what he was now doing. He looked toward the lake in a far-cast gaze. He had blanked his parents from his mind, but now confronted, it was difficult deciding what he thought about either of them.

He felt his body tense. He would not allow himself mordant sympathy. It was over. What was left was the discharge of the house, this token inheritance, this final reminder, and then it would be over. He closed his eyes, hoped to blank the house from his mind, but it lurked in his subconscious, the irony not lost that this house, which had been a source of great pain, had also been a source of great inspiration. In his first show, he had used an old-style projector with a carousel tray, rotating stock catalog images, the carousel click evidentiary in the slot of each image projected. It had proved a minor theatrical hit, the great burden thereafter, how to reproduce that success, to deviate from the voiceover and black box aesthetic. It was a challenge that had made him fitful and ill-tempered, fretful that his success had been a one-off.

ALONG THE dappled light on Sheridan Road, Joanne pointed to the palatial homes of those who had made it in Investments, Securities, and the Law. She slowed down, shielding her eyes against the midafternoon glare.

"You see all this, Grace? In America you can be anything you want to be."

Norman said, without turning around, "Joanne and I, we just didn't want to be."

Joanne scowled, "Don't tell a child that."

"Okay, let me clarify. We wanted it, but we couldn't get it."

Joanne looked into the rearview mirror. "Don't listen to him, sweetie." She directed her words toward Norman. "Why do you have to go tell her something like that? Her success is not based on whether we fail or succeed."

Norman was struck by the inclusive "we." He turned and said, "Daddy is just joking," so much of life compromise and biting your tongue. He was the problem, not Joanne. She was typical of an inducible hope tied to an Oprah-fashioned gospel of self-actualization and personal accountability. There was sometimes no point in defending the victims, they the most virulent and least open to understanding.

Joanne was suddenly excited. They were nearing Skokie. She announced that she had been here before. Yes, she had seen *Schindler's List* with her Loyola boyfriend at a major multiplex. She disconcertingly described how rows of "Jews" had sniffled their way through the movie, then asked Norman if he knew about the "forgotten Holocaust?" Her boyfriend was of Armenian heritage. Joanne added it by way of explanation. It explained a lot.

Of course, Norman knew about the forgotten Holocaust, but he pretended not to, allowing Joanne to fill in the scant details of what she had garnered from this boyfriend. Norman believed that this was how history was best come upon, the travails of heritage experienced in a depth of an empathy that had allowed Joanne and this boyfriend to get into each other's pants. Norman knew Joanne couldn't pick out Armenia on a map, but what interested him was how the profane and plain hurtful could be so wrapped up in such an apparent good-natured heart, because Joanne was all that, kind-hearted and strong, and nobody could deny it. She was, he understood, one of those daughters, who, under more pressing and simpler times, could be coaxed into believing almost anything about anybody and counted on to bear from her hips a race of madmen.

Norman kept his thoughts to himself. It had been an eventful morning, and yet they were out here at last at Joanne's insistence, Norman trying so very hard to be optimistic.

IN AN ENSUING QUIET of passing minutes, his phone buzzed. The realtor was postponing their meeting until late afternoon. Norman stared at the text. His inclination was to turn back, then he considered whether driving by the house might be enough. He was undecided. He was guarded in announcing the change in plans.

They drove on.

In a stalemate, Norman palmed his phone, scrolled to the story of Daniel Einhorn.

There were quotes from retirees who had lost everything, emotive stories of irrevocable loss. A victim had taken his own life. Another retiree was working at Walmart.

To Norman, all these sorts of stories did was sell newspapers, garnering a readership of collective indignation, when in reality, to Norman's way of thinking, everyone was indictable, the victims most definitely, beneficiaries of returns that were too high, so that surely they knew, and yet they had lured so many others, each wagering that they could make a killing and get out before it all collapsed.

Joanne asked, "Anything wrong?"

Norman looked up and answered, "No, it's all good," as Joanne, in the impropriety of wanting to see it, said, "What are you hiding?"

Norman relented, held the phone up as a part of full disclosure. He summarized the news story regarding Daniel Einhorn and the tragic losses. A bio described Einhorn as married and the father of two.

Joanne seemed struck by that fact. She said, "Kenneth was with . . ." then in looking at Grace, tempered the remark, substituting Kenneth with *he*, saying, "*He* was with a married man. . . . *Yuck* . . ."

Norman was alive to the double standard of her reaction. He might have said something, but he didn't.

Joanne asked, "You never did that, right?"

Norman refrained from answering. He directed his eyes toward Grace and then to Joanne in an indication that this wasn't a conversation that should be continued. He said to Grace, "We should get something to eat, right?"

Grace requested a milkshake.

Norman searched his phone. There was a Baskin-Robbins in Winnetka. He called out the directions.

Joanne, as yet unsettled by the revelation of Kenneth's involvement with a married man, looked at Norman and asked, "You knew *always* . . . what you were?"

Norman said stiffly, "You make it sound like a condition."

Chastened, Joanne got the message and said, "I'm sorry . . . okay?"

In the quiet indecision Norman opened the message from the realtor. He pretended it was a new message. He announced that the realtor had pushed the viewing back until the late afternoon. He added a lie, saying, "She says there's a potential client."

In a rallying vindication of having pressed that they view the house, Joanne said, "You see, coming out here got the realtor off her ass."

Grace said, "Ass . . . ," and Joanne, turning, said with feigned seriousness, "Language! Get off her tush! We don't say that other word."

Norman added, "Tush!" and then said with a display of unguarded openness, to reclaim the day, "We could go by Einhorn's house if you'd like, see how the other half lives. We're out here." He pulled up a shot of Einhorn as he said it.

Joanne said, "Woozers! That's Daniel Einhorn? What a hunk!"

Norman half smiled in the undertow of Joanne's essential directness. It lightened the moment, this the frank candor of two lost people.

Grace leaned forward, engaged in a way that she hadn't been previously, more aware than perhaps either gave her credit. She had undoubtedly heard the name Einhorn in the fights before Kenneth left, though she had never asked about Kenneth in his absence.

It was how her life had gone, the interchange of people in her life, or so Norman imagined it. He was glad of her presence, that he had somehow done something good, even if it had been initially for all the wrong reasons.

Ten

I N THE WINTRY LIGHT of midmorning, at the entrance to Lake
Forest Cemetery, what Nate Feldman noted was not the solemnity
of the cemetery but the large number of rules there, for a place where
only the dead resided.

It took time to find his father's grave. The newer part of the cemetery
was on a rolling tongue of hill, grave markers recessed into the grass.
Flowers and wreaths could not be left. It said so on a sign, an ordinance
that facilitated the living—namely, the grounds crew—in the expedient
sweep of their commercial-grade lawn mowers. When Nate eventually
found the grave, he scuffed the snow away with the toe of his shoe and
read the marker:

Theodore L. Feldman
Sgt
US Navy W W II
Sept 16 1922
Oct 19 1987
Beloved Husband & Father

Anyone walking through the graveyard would know that here lay a
man who had served in the line of fire when it was demanded. And yet
his father had found no valor in survival or, for that matter, in the act
of service. The postwar years had soured him, victory, short-lived. His
father had avoided the fetish of the dead, avoided the rousing sentiment
of a succession of Veterans Days, when a nation's thoughts were obliged
to settle on the collective heroism of all those who had passed, when, to
him, history and truth were always far more complex.

He said it one evening to Nate, coming to the perch of the carriage house out back of the main house. He had come out to call Nate in for supper. A panel on a TV show was debating the constitutionality of the draft. His father was decided, listening to it, that too much life had been lost in what he said Eisenhower had called the military-industrial complex. If the time came, there was the National Guard as a measure of last resort. His father had connections. It was the best of both worlds. Nate might serve and never see action. In the interim, there was life to be lived.

NATE ARRIVED AT his old house. He parked across the street. He stared at the carriage house where he had lived the last year of high school. His father had held old-fashioned views regarding relations between the sexes, a hijinks story of girls entering and exiting through a servants' door at the rear of the garage, his father attributing a salaciousness to Nate that was never the case. In reality, few girls visited, and yet his father swore that he knew all Nate's girlfriends by their perfume. He called them all "Duchess" and Nate "Swank."

When Nate's draft number came up in the fall of 1970, he decided not to seek a deferment. He told no one, not least his father, advancing on the idea of seeking his place in the world in the act of serving. It was the unpopular choice, but it carried with it a noble and gratifying significance. He did eventually confide his decision to his mother, begging her to say nothing to his father. A week later she betrayed him.

Nate heard his father shouting in the house. Time passed. Nate stood by the window. His father emerged eventually. He held a drink in his hand. Visibly drunk, he wavered, then advanced across the yard, entered the carriage house, and climbed the stairs.

Nate faced his father. His father dismissed the defiance. He didn't acknowledge that he knew about Nate's intentions. Instead, he leaned to set his scotch on a step, and then, rising, he showed how you strangled someone, declaring how he had strangled more than one gook with his bare hands during the war. That, he said, was what hand-to-hand combat was like, the Japs flushed island by island during the push through the fortified caves of Saipan and the lesser islands along the Marianas archipelago, the weapon of choice, the flamethrower.

What the Pacific theater had ended up being was a proving ground for Armageddon. He described how the Japs wouldn't surrender, so the bomb had to be dropped. There was no alternative. Each American had it settled in their hearts.

THEY WERE GOING on a fishing trip, Nate ceding to his father, Canada the alternative.

His father described how gear and supplies were meticulously packed and weighed in wartime. Canned provisions, a waxed canvas parka, wading boots, thermal underwear, a pocket knife, flint, a cache of dry kindling. His father weighed each item on a scale taken from the kitchen out in the yard.

To Nate, his father looked a version of his younger self, a ropey sinew about him, a leanness of a bygone era connected to the scarcity of a Great Depression that had honed a sort of strength measured in sit-ups, push-ups, and pull-ups—this what noble service had looked like at a point in American history—the fresh face of youth called forth in a willing sacrifice for values and ideals, in an uncomplicated truth shared by all.

Vietnam was different.

Through the early morning, Nate paced and waited. He saw his mother in the upstairs bedroom. A curtain moved, and she was gone from his life.

HE AND HIS FATHER talked once they were outside Chicago. According to his father, business had gone to hell. There had been mistakes at all levels of government. In fact, it wasn't about the American government anymore, but multinationals.

His father was then anticipating the rise of Japanese imports. He had a head for understanding the ways of the world, or maybe it was simply his hatred of the "Japs." It was hard reconciling what had been prophetic and what was hate. It was perhaps both. Whatever the case, for his father, the Vietnam War was a great distraction from what was really happening, the joke of Toyota and Honda four-stroke engines, compacts nobody in their right mind would drive and hadn't yet in any great numbers, but would eventually in a subtle narrowing of dreams, in rising oil prices and stagflation.

It was never about Nate. That was the cold truth that emerged on the journey.

Talk died between them beyond Gary, Indiana, with its belch of industrial smokestacks, in a complicated intersect of roads and semitrailers. Nate's father negotiated traffic, the car following the lower lobe of Lake Michigan. They eventually reached the dunes and summer homes serving Chicago weekenders, then pushed north toward isolation, falling temperatures, and Canada.

Nate closed his eyes, pretended to sleep, then did. He awoke to his father's hand on his shoulder. A truck approached. There was suspicion venturing north on roads like this. The truck passed, Nate's father eying it in his rearview mirror. He reached for and touched his hunting rifle with a reassurance that it was still there.

They pulled over a half hour later, the day given to a midwinter angle of yellowing light. Nate's father pissed in a desolate landscape and then zipped with an upward pull that straightened him at the spine.

Nate took a turn driving. All morning, his father had been sober, but he unscrewed a flask, took a long drink, wiped his mouth with the back of his hand, set the flask between his knees. The booze had its immediate effect, the reach of his father's words rising from currents that ran below political outrage.

They were heading north into ancestral territory, or so his father said. The Feldmans' height and jawline were linked to a Norwegian of immense beauty but petulant character, who had broken camp from a mirthless logging community and was bedded by a fur trapper named Feldman, so the Ingebrigtsen Norwegians, those lughead giants, had their bloodline infused by a sagacious taxidermist Jew from the Urals who knew something about fox fur and ermine and its value to the imperial court of czarist Russia.

When his father turned, his eyes were bloodshot with a boozy tiredness. He tendered a tremulous opinion that at a point in history, just before the Industrial Revolution, when men lived without the hitch of machines, when distances meant something, men had found the measure of their strength and temperament in nature, in lands yet uninhabited.

They passed into a thinning tree line of spruce and pine. His father stared into a depopulated world where one might again regain one's bearings. He drank, cradled the flask, his mouth agape like a fish.

He cleared his throat, loosening phlegm, alighting on the story of a great ox of a man, Per, their Norwegian primogenitor, who of his own volition, at age sixteen, left home, crossing Iceland and Greenland before making shore in North America. Per, a towering figure in the tradition of Paul Bunyan, found his eventual calling in what would become Minnesota, his passage to America secured through the Hudson's Bay Company, his landfall along a meandering river at a bleak outpost near Pictured Rocks on Lake Superior, where he was given the vague mandate to simply start chopping until someone came and got him. There was enough to keep him busy for a lifetime.

How his father knew these most intimate details was not up for debate. It was just understood that he did.

His father leaned against the door, wielded his arms as best he could in the act of swinging an ax. He described Per's strength, made a halted chop at something that could never be felled in a single blow, imagining the measured blows, impressing the absolute isolation. In those years of first discovery, he explained, men had lived rough, authentic lives, gathering in encampments at season's end. A breed apart, they were a sort that others did not willingly suffer to draw alongside, the comparison too striking in these giants' collective favor, so when camp broke, each giant went his separate way. In the clearing of the far north, so his father maintained, there were no stories of drunkenness or disaffection with life.

They were on a grey scratch of road.

His father drank, imagined Per, in the metronome swish of an axe, in advancing strides, coming upon a stream, slaking a summer parch, drinking like a horse, and at day's end, pitching a tent, flint struck against the coming dusk, a glow of kindling coaxed with a whisper, the sudden bloom of his shadow, his hand cupped like a teller of a great secret.

It was thus told, in the way stories are, for the listener—but for the teller, too, his father's days filled with an emptiness pit against a heroic life that never existed, which made it all the more irreconcilable, more tragic, because he believed it in his heart, and he would not be dissuaded that there was another way, when there never was.

By nightfall Nate left, his father by the fire, tucked knee to chest in a fitfulness of sleep and dreams.

NATE LOOKED UP. The morning had given way to early afternoon. He had been a day in America, and there were things still to be settled, not only with the dead, but with the living.

Back in his car, he took out his phone. He had used a private investigation agency to ensure that he had not been lured back onto American soil. It was a measure of caution. He was old and tired and not the man he had then been. He had been given a report, included in it, a file on Norman Price. He had learned that Price was under investigation for having potentially tried to blackmail Daniel Einhorn, a lover of Price's ex-partner. Nate had looked up Einhorn and deep into the report saw reference to where Einhorn lived—less than a mile from Nate's old home.

It struck him, the coincidence, and with it an awareness of how much the world had changed—the stolidity of his father's world swapped out for a new breed of financial shysters in the fallout of what his father had so long anticipated—the demise of American fortunes.

The details of the report on Norman Price seemed such a sordid, modern matter, the accusatory nature of a love gone bad, and then he read the reference to a child, a Chinese orphan. The world had undoubtedly changed.

He muttered it to Ursula, her spirit carried with him now in the way she wanted. He needed her strength, felt her divining presence in his having decided to venture home. He explained as best he could, remembering the hold she had on him, the grip of connections, the way she had sought his arms, his comfort, a smell of smoke in her hair.

He ventured toward Daniel Einhorn's home, drove by a wrought iron gate with a crested emblem of lion hearts. He observed a black Suburban, then fell in behind a car, the occupants a family of three, their heads turned, staring at the home. It was a fascination, what had been achieved under the guise of progress, when it had been all a great fraud. It drew people in, the way change might be upon America in the days of a new president and a new direction.

In the interest of things felt but never fully settled, Nate decided on contacting Norman Price. Helen Price had been at the center of a great mystery. He admitted it to Ursula, seeking her permission and guidance. He pulled over and wrote:

This is Nate Feldman. I am contacting you on the off chance you might remember my father, Mr. Theodore Feldman, longtime employer to your mother. I should be delighted to meet if you have the time.

Eleven

JOANNE PASSED Daniel Einhorn's home. There was a car parked across the street, a black Suburban with tinted windows, Norman believing that it was undoubtedly the FBI.

Joanne said to Grace, "The man who lives there, he did a very bad thing. He stole money from lots of people and now they have no homes. He's a *very* bad man."

Grace repeated, "He's a *very* bad man."

Joanne chimed in, encouragingly, "It's not nice to steal." Einhorn was proving to be a teachable moment. Joanne circled the block, passed the house again.

Norman shouted, "What the hell are you doing?" He literally ducked in his seat.

Joanne looked at him. "It's a free country. We're allowed to look."

Grace piped up. "Daddy's afraid of the *very* bad man, right, Daddy?" She touched Norman's shoulder in a gesture she had never before extended.

Norman righted himself, set his hand on Grace's. "Yes, Daddy is afraid of the very bad man."

Joanne added, "Well, Daddy's got his girls to protect him, right?"

It meant so very much to her. Norman understood it.

Joanne circled the block again. In her rearview mirror, she observed the slow progress of a car behind her, a lone driver. Norman also conscious of it, a pilgrimage of those come to observe a great wrong.

THEY WERE IN the heart of downtown Winnetka, a quaint village of an assortment of boutique stores—the exception, the franchise Baskin-

75

Robbins, though it was tastefully done in old-fashioned décor, with soda jerk high school kids serving, making it all the more intimate, this the first engagement in earning their own money.

Joanne and Grace were involved in careful deliberation, negotiating the thirty-three flavors of ice cream. An adolescent girl in an Izod working the counter thought Grace "the cutest thing ever."

They ate in a dalliance of a half hour, Grace advancing alone toward the ice cream. She wanted more free tastes. The girl in the Izod said the name of each flavor, scooped out samples. Grace licked each flavor, pocketing each plastic spoon.

The girl wanted to know how to say "ice cream" in Chinese.

Grace didn't know.

Norman piped up, "Communists don't have ice cream."

Joanne mock punched him.

Norman was steadfast. "They don't."

Joanne looked at him, asking, "Not even one flavor?"

Norman shook his head, and Joanne, raising her voice, said "Not even one flavor!"

When they were done, Joanne asked the girl if she drove yet, tendering a twenty-dollar bill and not wanting change on a nine-dollar order. The girl pocketed the twenty without comment. It turned out that the girl had been given a two-seater Jaguar for her sixteenth birthday, though she intimated that she was obliged to keep it washed as part of the deal.

Joanne smiled and said, without missing a beat, "That seems fair," Norman in full agreement that a sixteen-year-old deserved a Jaguar for her birthday.

Across the way, Joanne spotted a children's boutique. She announced that she and Grace were going shopping and that maybe Norman could just get a coffee. *Girls only!*

The girl overheard the conversation and said that there was a café down the street. Joanne smiled, glad of the intimacy, as though this life might be negotiated in civility and good manners, that this was where she truly belonged.

NORMAN ACQUIESCED, and at a small café ordered a double espresso. In a day waning toward a darkening sky, he saw beyond a tree line of oak and cedar the visible glow of city-light pollution, a bathing light belying an afternoon of falling temperatures and the gridlock of a treacherous afternoon commute. The longer they waited, the worse traffic would get.

A half hour had passed. Norman ordered another espresso. He had decided that they would go home. He would announce that the realtor was negotiating with an interested party, acknowledging that Joanne had been instrumental in advancing movement on the house, and that, in fact, she was right in most things.

Checking his phone, he was confronted by a text from Nate Feldman. He reflexively looked up, thinking that somehow Nate Feldman was sitting across from him, that he'd somehow been recognized. There was no Nate Feldman there. Norman checked the time stamp. It had been sent just over an hour ago. He couldn't shake the coincidence. He kept looking around. He read the message a second and a third time.

What struck him was the message's formal but ingratiating tone. The circumspect tone gave no indication as to the occasion or intent that prompted the message. It agitated Norman, the executive shorthand of a lording superiority, a goddamn Feldman summoning him with feigned deference.

He was tempted to delete the message. And yet he didn't. He did a search for Nate Feldman and came across the sale of Grandshire Organics for $15.5 million. The article, dated April 11, 2002, listed Nate Feldman as founder and CEO. There was no reference to Nate's being American. Norman didn't want to believe it, but it was Nate Feldman, an inserted photograph incontrovertible evidence, Nate, the image of his father.

Norman closed the text. It was near too much to bear. Goddamn success followed these people! He felt a rush of shame, a sullen insurmountable fact facing him, of what he was and who the Feldmans were, and how easy it had been for his mother to choose! It was there again, an insistent memory, the weight of all that had passed in those early years of his life. He remembered Mr. Feldman calling him Fauntleroy on the occasions Helen brought him to the office, Norman made to dress in a get-up of blazer and slacks because Mr. Feldman liked snappy dressers, while Helen never failed to make mention of Norman's grades, straight As. It was a tradition of sorts.

The condescension of the name Fauntleroy burned a hole through Norman. The grades had always proved an overture for a toast, Mr. Feldman pouring a measure of scotch, another for Norman and for Helen, announcing, "To Fauntleroy!," downing his, then swooping to drink Norman's shot and what remained of Helen's before bustling them to lunch at his club; the report card always set on the table as evidence of a burgeoning mind, and where at some point in the charade, the maître d' arrived, held the report card to the light to make sure it wasn't a forgery, and satisfied it was not, dutifully informed Fauntleroy that when he came of age, there was room for him at The Club. In the immediate aftermath, always Norman panicky that his name be rightly taken down, would tell Helen to tell them. He was Norman, not Fauntleroy—the absolute gullibility, the goddamn bravado of Mr. Feldman and the complicity of Helen!

It was alive again, those emblazoned days of the city's grandeur, the velvet fall of draped curtains, cigars and brandy, set against Walter's arrival home with a Dutch apple crumble picked from the discount rack on the occasion of all As.

Norman had included a soliloquy in *Confessions of a Latchkey Kid*, a disconsolate memory of Walter's wrapping him in a blanket for a drive out to Winnetka in a quiet surveillance, Helen supposedly working overtime for Mr. Feldman at his carriage house, the car filled with the smell of Heinemann's cinnamon strudel and black coffee, Norman remembering the crinkling give of a foil container against a plastic knife, Walter cutting strudel, handing a slice into the dark.

THERE WAS ANOTHER TEXT, this from the realtor. There had, in fact, been an interested buyer, or so said the realtor, communicating the upshot of a dismal showing. Her recommendation was that Norman sink funds into the house. The dining room off the kitchen was too small, too dated, and there was something obviously wrong with the plumbing. The realtor included the number of a licensed plumber.

Norman was cognizant that the realtor had probably never been to the house, that she had arrived in advance and, finding it unsatisfactory, was now tendering this advice. There had been no client. He understood that he had been too guarded and remote in not dealing directly with the realtor, that Joanne was right, that he should have met up with her long ago if simply to impress his interest in wanting the house sold.

Looking up, Norman saw Joanne advance across the street. Grace was in tow, dressed in a wool blazer, pleated tartan skirt, white ankle socks, and patent leather Mary Janes.

Joanne smiled as she entered the café. She slipped Norman a primrose-colored envelope with a raised seal containing the receipt. She made Grace pirouette like a figure on a music box, declaring, "Doesn't she look beautiful!"

There was no denying her exoticness.

In the outfit, Grace looked to Norman like a character from a children's book. *Madeline* came to mind. Norman kept looking at her, observing the cardboard cutout of her features, the flat face and the slanted eyes, the composite shorthand identifying features a good illustrator could turn into a signature series. He was mindful, too, of the precocious child protagonist of the *Clifford the Big Red Dog* series, living on a coastal New England island of white privilege.

And then the question surfaced, why couldn't he do the same? A compendium of *Grace & Randolph* books—*Grace & Randolph Learn the Hard Truth about China's One Child Policy*; *Grace & Randolph Get Undercut in the Lemonade Stand Business and Learn Hard and Fast Truths about Outsourcing*; *Grace & Randolph Learn about Derivatives and Futures and Why Daddy Won't Sleep with Mommy Anymore and Is Banging the Secretary*.

He knew his main problem had always been having too large a vocabulary and having too much to say. It was anathema for an artist. Maybe he could go with a Chinese alphabet book, be ahead of the curve in the insipid way parents were now anticipating the reality of what was fast approaching—the decline of the West.

A CLUTCH OF elderly women quietly assessed Grace. Norman caught their eye as one of the elderlies volunteered her granddaughter was learning Chinese. She gave Norman an obliging smile. It was obvious that they had been disparagingly wondering which of them had the reproductive problem, Norman or Joanne.

A man in a yellow cashmere sweater and tomato red pants came across to their table with affable familiarity. Norman had not noticed him before. He gave off a new-car smell. His name, Roger Carlyle. He was in real estate. His face was on his business card. That seemed to be his essential credential, a face.

Norman watched Roger give Joanne the once-over, assessing who controlled the purse strings, Norman witnessing the spark of intrigue the two engendered in one another. It let him understand something about Joanne, about the sort of man she might let enter her life.

Roger wondered whether Grace would like to record the Pledge of Allegiance on his iPhone. It was something he did for anybody who bought a house.

Joanne chimed in that they *had* a house on the market. Maybe Roger knew the realtor?

Norman understood that she had no clue where the house was and was equally oblivious to the demarcation of towns along the North Shore, and with it, an inveterate snobbery.

The house was, in fact, further north. Norman said the name. Yes, Highwood, a shithole enclave amidst the splendor of Highland Park and Lake Forest, Highwood pushed up against the lake, a town historically linked to military recruits in what had once been the active military base of Fort Sheridan, Highwood, complete with its military police, its down-market bars and tattoo parlors, its lifeline economy now inextricably tied to immigrant lawn care businesses serving the surrounding towns.

Joanne prattled on. She admitted that Grace didn't know the Pledge of Allegiance.

Roger had lost interest. It was evident to Norman. Self-conscious shame burned within him. There was no sale here, and yet Joanne made Grace go stand before Roger, who proved a sport, Roger conceding that most kids didn't know the pledge. He had the words in a pdf. He continued the charade. He did it for the elderly ladies watching. They, too, had heard the word "Highwood." This was charity, droppings from the manor extended to those below, or Norman felt it.

Roger wanted to send the file to Joanne, who looking at Roger mouthed that Grace was not yet reading. Not to be dissuaded, Roger said that Joanne and Grace could read it together.

It was too much for Norman. He intervened and asked, "*The Breakfast Club* was filmed here, and *Home Alone*?"

Roger Carlyle declined to engage.

Norman pressed. "And *Ferris Bueller's Day Off*, right? John Hughes' existential masterpiece of adolescent disaffection that asks the really hard question facing all of us, 'What the *fuck* will we do with the rest of our lives?'"

They left in a bustle of commotion, Joanne so suddenly taken by the outburst, Roger Carlyle and the clutch of elderlies equally mortified.

Joanne hustled Grace across the road. When they got to the car, Joanne glared at Norman and screamed, "You asshole! You ruin everything!"

Norman demanded the keys. He wouldn't suffer the indignity of being the passenger. Roger Carlyle was in the street, his phone to his ear, talking and walking, advancing on the car, trying to discern the license plate.

Norman abruptly pulled away from the curb as a police cruiser approached. It passed, and in a wheeling turn, was suddenly behind them, its lights swirling, lighting up the interior of the car.

Twelve

NORMAN SPOKE TO Joanne on a payphone in the single call allowed. Her voice was a rush of emotion. They weren't telling her anything. The car was impounded. She didn't understand why. It didn't make sense. Her voice was on the verge of hysteria. Norman was circumspect in detailing the charges against him. Joanne needed to contact Kenneth. He had a home number for Kenneth's father on his computer. Joanne should call it. He didn't explain why.

The call lasted less than two minutes before Norman was cut off.

JOANNE BOARDED a downtown bus. Grace was still in the purchased outfit. They sat in the rear of the bus. Joanne held Grace's hand. It had all so suddenly ended, what had been a day of prospects and high hope. Joanne staved off tears. She felt a stab of a betrayal. She had misunderstood Norman's motivation. She knew in calling Kenneth's father she was likely ending what she had salvaged these last few months. There was something unsaid, some implication regarding Norman, Einhorn, and Kenneth, something that warranted police involvement. She had been shut out of an unfolding secret.

Joanne took a deep breath. How could this be happening, and all she had done. She had tried so very hard. And now it was gone.

Grace roused, opened her eyes, but closed them again.

Joanne let her hand rest on Grace's forehead. She stared into the night. She was back to where she had been New Year's Eve, at the precipice of boarding a bus back to Buffalo and landing on Sheryl and Dave's door. She felt a rush of humiliation, the concatenation of lost chances with potential men, her desperation apparent in her aloneness, in all she had been through. Among the men, a lawyer, David Croft, who for a time had held such promise, a heartbreak that she had not revealed to Norman. David Croft was in his second year with a major law firm when she met him. She was working at a bookstore on Michigan Avenue, managing a section of coffee table books with lavish prints of the great masters, marketed to an upscale clientele with skyrise waiting rooms.

David arrived one day, brown-bagging a lunch, at ease with life, his tie loosened. Working in the art section had bestowed an intelligence on her, or she thought David thought so. It had emboldened her. She had been required to learn and then casually reference historical influences or stylistic innovations of the great masters. It moved stock in a subtle handselling. One lunch hour, she brought him collected volumes of Monet, Renoir, and Cézanne, and in a gesture of advancing boldness, another time, a book of Gauguin's postimpressionist French Polynesian period, the book opened to the image of two Tahitian beauties titled *When Will You Marry?* as she explained how a flower behind the ear signaled availability for marriage.

A month into their relationship, he took her with the tenderness of a man seeking something more meaningful than a passing girlfriend. There had been all the right signals. There was a getaway during an important case along the Michigan shoreline, a lake cottage secured by his great-grandfather during the Depression. She listened and he talked, recounting a dormitory extension of functional bunks, an entanglement of limbs and advancing youth, a grit of sand on everything, a clothesline strung with bathing suits.

There was nothing in the inventory of it suggesting anything other than that he had loved her. In a window out back of the cottage, he pointed to Chicago across the lake, this what his immigrant great-grandfather had claimed against a life working in Chicago's slaughterhouses. It meant something to him, this legacy. He was affected by tradition and family, connected with a parsimony of money saved by immigrants and with the opinion that the further a people moved from that source of want, when they didn't know hunger and deprivation, the further a society was sunk and in decline. He was talking about America, but also his life, and she thought he might be a Supreme Court justice for the interest he had in the grander sense of how life might be lived and arbitrated.

And then, right on the mark of six months, he swapped her out for a fellow lawyer, a former classmate with a sparrow's face and pinched lips and half his height. Joanne had agonized over points of difference, when it made not a whit of difference, when it wasn't any one thing. She cried reading their engagement announcement.

GRACE WAS fitful in sleep. She stirred but didn't wake. Joanne watched her, this child who had become so much the center of her life. Was this to be taken from her? She struggled thinking it, used the heel of her hand against her nose, moving toward a call she would have to make to Kenneth's father. And after it was done, she would call Sheryl and Dave. She had a sympathetic understanding of what it took to survive. She was open to forgiveness and reconciliation, but they, of course, wouldn't be.

Thirteen

Daniel Einhorn didn't sleep with his wife anymore. It happened without argument, part of the natural evolution of a relationship that had diverged along the way. He stared at a cycle of feeds on a home security system and, zooming in, stopped on his wife's bedroom. A TV threw a shifting light, so there was apparent movement, a rumor of life, when it was her alone, fast asleep. It upset him greatly, in the way Jesus in the Garden of Gethsemane had chided Peter to stay awake. Elaine had benefited from all that had been perpetrated. He was tempted to rouse her, felt it would happen soon, Saul Herzog's henchmen coming for him.

In pajamas and bare feet, Einhorn was like a penitent come a long and difficult path.

Kenneth Birch was dead. Two bullets had been fired into the back of the head, an execution style killing reminiscent of the manner in which Saul had so often described how Einhorn would most likely die. Kenneth, it turned out, had tried to blackmail Saul Herzog.

Einhorn learned this on a phone call at his office and, hanging up, knew his life was over, but it was not unexpected.

FOR THE BETTER PART of a decade Einhorn had been watching his back, the secret trysts in hotels in the late afternoon, the complicated sequence of heading to the health club, changing for a leisurely run, and ending up literally running to a hotel room for hours lost here and there. It was a sexual awakening that might have been tolerated and managed under different circumstances. The world was an enlightened place. At issue was not Einhorn's sexuality but Saul's essential hold on him. Einhorn didn't conceivably have a life without Saul Herzog. They were too deep in a fraud that could not see any break in the ranks.

Einhorn knew in his heart that he had been a handpicked scapegoat, chosen three decades ago, purposely for his loose-ended family, for his expendability when the time came, though Saul had lauded Einhorn, made pretense of his holding great sway and power within the family, because it would be needed in whatever defense Saul eventually mounted.

Einhorn's relationship with Elaine Herzog dated to a Fourth of July party at the Herzogs' during the deregulatory zeal of the Reagan administration, Einhorn then interning with Sachs. Elaine, a twenty-eight-year-old debutante, had studied psychology and was at a loose end. Saul put them together, Einhorn understanding Elaine was part of the package being offered, and if Elaine was mindful of it, she never let on. Love didn't figure in the Herzog household—life tied to a series of mergers and acquisitions, so why should love fall outside the domain of practical interests? In this way, Einhorn became part of family gatherings centered on tradition and ceremony, a rabbi blessing each gathering, there for the equanimity of moral guidance, the house peopled with men of means and all willing to invest.

Businesswise, Einhorn had the instincts to leverage and manipulate information just shy of criminality. He could close on a deal. Saul admired these qualities. It wasn't simply that Einhorn was a patsy. For years, he was Saul's right-hand man, Einhorn capable of extending the family's business interests, Saul grooming what was essentially there. As Saul put it, a hypnotist could not make a man do what he didn't want to, but a hypnotist could call upon what was within a person, and Saul, a reader of the Old Testament, falling upon the story of Daniel, who put his head in the mouth of a lion, and how it required great faith, and that he, Saul, could tell Einhorn had come from a people who were used to putting their heads in the mouths of lions.

Saying that, Saul was the most charismatic and calculating character Einhorn would ever know, Saul and his kind, old hands at history, survivors of the rise and fall of empires, the Roman, the Byzantine, the Ottoman, and a scourge of countless pogroms. They had experienced the best and the worst of times, been roused, beaten, and dragged from their homes, starved and kicked around Europe, and then they had found America and Wall Street.

ON THE AFTERNOON of Einhorn's engagement to Elaine, Saul had insisted they meet in advance of dinner at the baths at the Union Club. When Einhorn arrived, Saul was in the company of a gracious Czech named Pavel Matějček, a valet wearing a white smock.

Pavel and Saul were fast friends. Since his arrival in America, Pavel had spent his days folding towels and robes, filling up plastic cups with mouthwash, setting out talcum powder and deodorant for the members of the Union League Club. Pavel affirmed certain truths for Saul—namely, that the poor were necessarily dependent on the rich for their livelihood, and the best of them understood this.

It was perhaps Pavel's greatest gift, why he was still alive when others had been less fortunate under Soviet occupation, and yet in America, for all his abiding belief in free markets, Pavel Matějček would eventually lose everything to Saul's Ponzi scheme. In fact, it was partly Pavel's money that was paying for dinners and expenses on which Pavel never would have dreamed of spending money.

Saul had been telling a joke—Saul, who could and did tell the most subversive of jokes, usually about his own people, which made it all the more scandalous and unnerving. Saul began again, for Einhorn's sake, and for two other fat men who appeared and were given towels by Pavel.

"Moscow, in deepest winter. A rumor spreads through the city that meat will be available the next day at a butcher's shop. Hundreds arrive. They carry stools, vodka, and chessboards. There is great excitement. At 3 A.M., the butcher comes out and says, 'Comrades, the Party Central Committee called. It turns out there won't be meat for everyone. Jews go home.' The Jews leave. The rest continue to wait. At 8 A.M., the butcher comes out again: 'Comrades, I've just had another call from Central Committee. It turns out there will be no meat at all. You should all go home.' The crowd disperses, grumbling all the while, 'Those bloody Jews, they get all the luck!'"

A CAR MOVED ACROSS the crackle of a loose stone drive. The gate opened from within. There was only Elaine home. It was happening as though it had been planned for a long time, which it had.

Einhorn hid inside his daughter's walk-in cedar closet with the mordant understanding that this was how it happened in horror movies, so the only option was the closet when the monster was in the house.

After Saul had seen him take the call, Einhorn had gone down to the mail room and hastily written a note to his lawyer, providing the location of a key in his Chicago Union Club locker. His lawyer was to give the key to Einhorn's daughter, Rachel, to whom he wrote a separate note, telling her to use the key at Chicago First National. A safe-deposit box there contained a stash of money, along with bonds that could be discreetly accessed, and that if she spent wisely, if she stayed below the radar of the IRS, if the sum of her purchases were not too extravagant, when the IRS stopped looking, when the present scourge of accountability passed, she might resume life in its natural order, in which there would always be a separation of the rich from the poor. Einhorn was no snob in thinking it, aligned with how even Jesus conceded that the poor would always be among us, so the Almighty could live with around 7 percent unemployment, this, the best that could be hoped for in an imperfect world.

He shut the door behind him and stood amidst Rachel's clothes. She was now married. He stared at the rows of imported cashmere, Izods in pastel colors and popup collars no longer in fashion, the obscene number of dresses, shoes, boots, sneakers, and sandals, all in their original boxes, never worn, or worn once. In their totality, these items suggested that a great fraud had been committed, the way Imelda Marcos and her three thousand pairs of shoes had sparked true moral outrage in a world grown too accustomed to mass graves.

What Daniel Einhorn had to do was not believe most things said about him and his kind, protect his daughter by surrounding her with children of like-minded fraudsters, enrolling her at a day school, where she measured what she had against those who had as much, or more, so she could say without reproach, "Why don't we have what they have?"

They were not easily understood, the feelings of the privileged, but each could and did feel a genuine hurt that, at times, life wasn't turning out as it should, that there were things as yet beyond their reach, that $60 million was in fact not nearly enough money, so the hurt of a child, no matter how misguided, was still a genuine hurt, and that the children were essentially blameless and needed unequivocal protection. They were victims who didn't seem like victims, and when justice was meted out, they were the ones most often scorned, while they were a symptom and not the problem itself.

He might have begun his defense thus, in the relative comparison to what others had—well, not the majority, but in relation to those who mattered. He could not account for those who had few aspirations and even less drive, for it was an undeniable fact that despite what it said in the Declaration of Independence, all men were not created equal. He believed this in his heart—not that men could not aspire to greatness, but most did not. That was a crime in itself. Nothing had come easy.

EINHORN WAS AGAIN in the hallway. He walked to his office. Let them find him in the act of uploading or downloading a file, doing something suspicious and unnerving and deserving of his fate. Let Saul's men kill him in his leather chair in his home. It held a certain appeal. The alternative, nightmarish, to be taken, executed, dismembered, and fed piecemeal to hogs at the farm Saul owned in the Wisconsin Dells.

Fourteen

NATE WAS UP EARLY, at five in the morning, for a midmorning appointment with the law office of Weatherly, Sutherland, and Saunders. There were documents needing his signature in advance of the release of the reels.

He checked his phone for a reply from Norman Price. There was none.

He had slept at a Comfort Suites, set amidst a professional complex of financial services that had sprung up around a tax code that could be leveraged with the acumen of financial planners to cover the spread of the market and where, for the better part of two decades, you could anticipate a 20 percent return on investments. Money made money.

The buffet breakfast included not just orange juice and Danish pastries, but baskets of multigrain breads, yogurts, and an array of fresh-cut fruit, along with waffles and scrambled eggs. America had its largesse still, the reach of commerce smoothing over the underlying realities of the exponential divide between rich and poor. It was said everywhere, yet it was difficult seeing it or even intuiting it. These were grave and troubling times, but great also in the comparison across the ages, in how the Great Depression unfolded and left so many with nothing. This was of equal proportionality, perhaps greater, but it didn't seem that way.

Nate scanned a complimentary *USA Today*, finished breakfast, then went down past a fitness center. It had a galactic feel of self-improvement in the gleam of futuristic equipment. An infinity pool, like a bead of mercury, floated in an effervescent shimmer, suggesting a lightness without boundaries, divesting one of certain nostalgias, auguring home might be configured anywhere, anyplace, a seductive idea after all he had been through, in the memory of yesterday. Home in the distant future lived afloat in unmoored space, aboard the colossus of interstellar vessels crossing the void.

Nate saw existence better in the moment, what true history revealed, deep emptiness, and not the clutter of experiences and places that grounded and held him. There was something to Ursula and Frank Grey Eyes's way of seeing the universe. It stalked him still, the memory of his father, the inlaid plated memorial out there, less than two miles away from where he was now standing. He resisted the idea of going there again, then did at six in the morning in advance of dawn, the sky a blue dark.

He walked toward his father's grave, somnambulant as a ghost, a disembodied spirit wandering, and standing unannounced, felt the almost real sense he could resurrect his father. A hurt persisted. It was in his heart and head, all that his father represented, the unfathomable reach of his history, the burden of having been the son of Theodore Feldman.

He knew the story. His father was brought up outside St. Cloud, Minnesota, how he clawed his way out, earned a scholarship to Cornell in New York, enrolled in ROTC, wore his uniform exclusively because he had no respectable civilian clothes, and compensated the way certain men could turn disadvantage to advantage. His father, unabashed in revealing these personal details at any number of company speeches, speaking of himself exclusively in the third person, describing this and that about a young Theodore Feldman, resolute in announcing what a good attitude could achieve. Nate was present at one such speech.

In reality, his father was different in private. To the outside world, by all accounts, Nate Feldman had lived in the shadow of a small greatness, the son of a father given to the execution of duty, responsible for the lives of so many, first in war and then in business. His father, in his aloneness, in the decommission of a day's end, drank and was neither given to compliment nor compassion, lost to a blur of days that eventually could not be ignored.

It had been a slow death, long in coming, different from how an animal might die. He was talking in a way Ursula might, letting her see this world through his eyes, seeking the register of the right metaphor. He remained at the grave, hesitant, awaiting some clarifying sense of under-standing. What had his father bequeathed him? It was so patently typi-cal of his father, these reels, what they might reveal, handled through the administrative execution of his secretary. At a point, everything passed through Helen Price.

A hoary frosting on the graveyard made it look not so much a grave-yard but a golf course. His father might have appreciated the irony. He had favored golf as the modern incarnation of a hushed containment of how the world might yet be recouped, golf coming closest to the digni-fied reach of what American greatness could maintain after the turmoil of two world wars, a refinement of the links courses of Scotland, reenvi-sioned as a more attenuated game played along the sunbaked peninsula of Florida and up through the swelter of Augusta and out in the dry desert of Palm Springs. This, his father believed, was how you reori-ented a society, set the quiet bounds of restriction within the greater illusion of a democracy. You set a man like Arnold Palmer out there. His father so greatly admired Palmer for the far reach of his tee shot, a ball sailing along the fairway, the entire gallery following with hushed admiration, knowing it should, or would, land, and most always did, within ten yards of what was expected—his father proud America could offer the world a man of such distinguished character and grace: Palmer, a man comfortable in the bosom of democracy, walking among specta-tors. The British Empire had fallen because of snobs and bores with the great imperial condescension of its subjects, and here was Palmer, a new man for a new age; a man among men.

What his father had liked was the keen sense of the predictable: Palmer, conferring intent with eye contact to his club-laden caddy, sug-gesting a six iron on the approach shot, then proceeding against the microbial swell of the crowd, arriving eventually at the velvet texture of a green that called for a more deliberate read of the way the lines broke, the wide arc of Palmer's putt improbably breaking toward the hole along a line of sight only Palmer could read. And then the tempered applause, Palmer waving politely to the crowd, while, in the offing, the prospect of a well-made drink awaited, poured by a good-natured Negro at the clubhouse, a clubhouse where neither Negroes nor women alike were ever going to become members. There were simply bounds that needed to be kept.

It was easy to analyze history, to see a grave and assess a life, when the dull stuff of everyday life disappeared, leaving the subconscious to decide what was worth keeping.

Fifteen

JOANNE WOULD NOT admit it, but on hearing that Kenneth was dead, her first emotion—no, her second—was tremulous relief. She regretted thinking it. In the father's voice, she listened to a halted reckoning with decisions made and certain inevitabilities. The call lasted three minutes.

TWENTY MINUTES PASSED in a deadening silence. The phone was in her lap. She dialed.

Peter answered on the second ring.

Joanne asked, "What's it like, Oklahoma?" She had heard Oklahomans were called "Sooners," but she never looked up its meaning.

Peter obliged. The Sooners were so-called because some jumped *sooner* than the official start time for the race in the state's opening of free land.

Joanne said, "I suppose the others are called the 'Laters'?"

Peter was in between grading papers. He turned a paper. Joanne heard the sound.

Snow was falling. He described it, how winds blew unimpeded across the plains, creating whiteouts and drifts. Roads could disappear just like that.

Joanne closed her eyes. She could see it, the vastness—the emptiness, their talk a series of words hitched to dislocated loneliness.

Peter explained how the Board of Regents was investigating an online college program, the most desolate places often in need of the greatest advancements. If you were injured in Oklahoma, chances were you would be flown by helicopter to a regional facility, your scans read by somebody in Oklahoma City or Tulsa or, maybe, not even by an

American or even read in America, the Great Plains a great contradiction of patriotism and pragmatism. It was all monoculture and great machines, robotic harvesters controlled from satellites. They kept the rodeos alive for a sense of nostalgia, but most rode a mechanical bull in the bars on a Friday and Saturday night.

In simply speaking, Peter pushed an alternative reality on her. He didn't say which was better. He did the majority of the talking.

PETER WAS LIVING with the widow of a farmer who had died while riding atop a great combine harvester that covered nearly twenty miles of planted wheat after he died. The farmer had been found a county over, in wheat so high that they had to follow the trail left in his wake, working backward to discover where he most probably died.

It was patently absurd. Joanne said nothing. "Farmer" was the farmer's name, which was equally suspicious. Peter's greatest failing had always been beginning with the incredible, not accounting for the ordinary stuff of life that might have better served him. She might have said it, conferred something that she had thought for a long time. She didn't. It was none of her business, not anymore.

Peter set about reciting a poem that he had written about the death of George Farmer. The poem, titled "Silo . . . ," was pronounced Sigh Low. He was playing with some literary effect. It was a poem not for the page but to be read aloud, with a lot of alliteration and onomatopoeia, or some such literary inventiveness.

Joanne checked on Grace. Randolph roused.

She hushed him and went back into the hallway.

There were, according to Peter, communities out in Oklahoma preparing for the apocalypse and believed it was fast approaching.

Joanne had the insistent urge to bake something. She gathered ingredients in the kitchen, Peter all the while describing a concatenation of details, how Jessie met George Farmer at the Federal Building, where McVeigh had killed all those people. Farmer, Peter said, had been handing out plastic books of psalms, and he had asked Jessie to pray for those lost.

Joanne said, "You should write all this down now, not to forget it," even self-centered Peter alive to a growing desperation and fanatism, with his George and Jessie Farmer.

Joanne felt Norman's influence in his office. She could see his white board in his office, the grand connective sense of everything evident, if one looked hard enough, if one sought the truth, and she might have added to it, what was in full swing up in Upstate New York, Dave and Sheryl, both of them living with the confirmed belief that they were living through a world come undone by "commies, blacks, and *A-rabs*," and that a legitimate alternative might be for Dave to pump a round of ammo into Sheryl, Misty, and the boys' heads, then off himself with an abiding belief that life might resume under better conditions in the Afterlife. It was an alternative reached by more people than one wanted to admit.

Joanne rolled out her dough, pressed on the cookie cutter to shape gingerbread men. She made a sad-faced effigy gingerbread man of Peter. She could almost transpose what was being said in her ear as something communicated by the gingerbread man. And she had the curious thought of what might it be like to pull an arm off—one, then the other, and the legs, too, anything to stop him.

Sixteen

MR. AHMET WAS an old-world figure, swarthy, small in stature, and made smaller by recent illness. The wrinkles around his eyes suggested an ingrained, inky darkness of indeterminate immigrant stock, Middle or Far Eastern, anywhere from Turkey to Uzbekistan. He bore the prosecutorial aesthetic of a minor bureaucrat from a Kafka novel.

He was forthcoming, slow and deliberate in choosing his words. He had been legal counsel and advised the four officers in the alleged gangland murder of the two drug dealers, and he had known Walter very well, right from the beginning of the lamentable and deplorable case and down through the years.

It turned out Walter's case and that of the other four had been Mr. Ahmet's longest and most complex, a watershed case when the city had begun changing its view of how policing was conducted. He explained it. He had been hired because of civil rights advances and affirmative action. It was what interested him in the law, how righteousness could eventually prevail. He was given to moments of self-reflection and, shaking his head, saying how the years had passed, and so quickly.

Mr. Ahmet continued. He had made a great many friends in defending those who needed defending on the force. It had been his honor, advising and helping with the case. He stated it like he was giving a sworn statement.

The system, he conceded, was utterly corrupt, or had been rife with a demoralizing cronyism for years, but such were the times, and a man had a right to survive as best he could and to make compromises. He understood the ways of the world. It was important to understand a man's motivations and proceed from there. His index finger touched the desk as he enumerated points along a history of his career and his own principles. His voice held a directness, suggesting English was not his first language. He came upon words, chose them. He spoke in complete sentences.

MR. AHMET WAS DONE with his own introduction. Retrieving a pair of wire-rimmed glasses, he placed the wire around first the left ear and then the right. His interest was in a box on the table. He began thumbing through folders. When he looked up, his eyes were magnified.

He said directly, "This Daniel Einhorn, to whom you sent that unfortunate letter. He is missing. Early this morning. His wife called. She was at the house. She claims to have heard nothing."

Mr. Ahmet peered over the rim of the box. "Can you imagine, a house that big, and your wife not knowing where you are? What a luxury! My wife, she accuses me of speaking like an old Marxist. She would love a house as big as Daniel Einhorn's house. I am sure of it, but everything comes at a great cost."

Mr. Ahmet's glasses were at the end of his nose. He landed on a summative assessment. "I am sure this Mr. Einhorn is most probably dead. There is, no doubt, a story there somewhere. Maybe you will write about it?"

Norman said, against his own interest, "I don't write about crime."

Mr. Ahmet's myopic eyes fixed on Norman. "Ah, yes, you indict on more ambiguous charges. I am aware of your *talents*, of course."

Norman answered stiffly. "I don't deal in bodies . . . in a body count." He revised his remark. "As a writer, I am in search of a suspicion of happiness."

Mr. Ahmet removed his glasses. "Yes, I know, and such lofty ideals. My sister-in-law, if I may tell you, she is the one in the family with the brains, but she will make a thing complicated when it need not be. She is a Mr. Woody Allen fan. She likes the sort of movie you just described, where there's 'a suspicion of happiness . . .' She has been through two husbands and many lovers. She is a very scandalous and independent woman. Little satisfies her, but I have said to her most times unease— bad conscience—is tied to bad acts. This is proof, I said to her when it was learned what this Mr. Woody was alleged to have done, sleeping with his daughter, or the adopted daughter of his wife. This Mr. Woody, with the twitching face of a watchmaker's son, but perhaps, if you can make your pathology, your perversions and insights, into something others want to pay to see, that's a definition of a kind of art."

Norman flushed. "If this is about me being gay . . ."

Mr. Ahmet waved off the suggestion. "This is the problem your father talked about, your perception that the world is against you! I went to see one of your shows. What I will say is that all artists should know the story of others as much as their own. As legal counsel, this is what I am tasked with every day. Where are your sympathies for others? You cannot dig half a hole. That is what I suspect you have been digging all these years!"

Mr. Ahmet continued. "If I may, I could tell you about real discrimination! My parents and I, we are immigrants. When we arrived in Chicago, we found the Irish, the Italians, and the Poles had it sewn up between them. The Irish and their famine, it is known throughout the world, and yet they held power in the city like they had never known hardship. My parents, when they arrived, came to understand America was not what they had expected, but they had lived through the alternative. We left on the backs of donkeys."

Mr. Ahmet crossed his heart. "By the time I got to high school, I was ambitious. I announced I wanted to be a lawyer. My parents, they said, 'Ahmet the lawyer, ridiculous!' They spat it, like it was a curse. They had their religion, their community. They had endured Stalin and the purges. I remember the Child of Prague visiting our church for a week of devotionals and how we went for the absolution of our sins, prayed to a doll in an ermine coat for favor and blessings. Such extravagance, the doll in a gold tabernacle, ferried cross-country in a short school bus used more commonly to transport those with a mental retardation. What I am saying, I was ashamed of my heritage. Enlightenment can do something to a person that is good, but also injurious."

Norman added, "But you became a lawyer?"

Mr. Ahmet nodded. "Yes, I became a lawyer, but first a night court clerk and then, much, *much* later, law school. I met a stenographer at the county courthouse. I fell in love and married in the most reckless of ways, a divorced woman with two boys, a second-generation Romanian with hair black as coal. "The Gypsy," my parents called her. The sacrifices they had made. I went on supporting them. At forty-four, I was the oldest graduate. I was a laughingstock. My parents, they said, 'Ahmet the lawyer, ridiculous!' I was in a cap and gown and in a great amount of debt, and all my parents wanted to know was what money I might have made if I had just worked and not studied. They were, of course, right, but money is not everything. Dignity and satisfaction count in ways that cannot be measured. They could not appreciate it. You stop learning or your understanding of the world ends at a certain point. I was their son and not their son. I became a married man, a husband, a father, and then a lawyer. My father, regrettably, he remained all his life a goatherder, or, more tragically, an ex–goat herder, and my mother, the wife of an ex–goat herder. It takes a generation perhaps. They had found the courage to leave, but the language was a great obstacle, and in the end, I broke free and had my own life. It is the same already, with my sons, and now my grandsons. It begins with the music they listen to. That is how you know when life has passed you by."

In this appraisal, there was a connected sense of why Mr. Ahmet was here, that it connected to a view of parents. Norman simply waited.

IT WASN'T ESTABLISHED why so much information had been gathered in the box related to Walter's suicide and his killing of his wife. There would be no case, and yet it was evident a great deal of time had been given to establishing a timeline related to Walter's last day alive. The writing on each folder was all the same hand, a looping cursive, Norman understanding it was Mr. Ahmet's work alone.

Mr. Ahmet began with a review of Helen's movements on the day of the accident, captured in still photographs by a series of street cameras. In a photograph, Helen's car passed her oncologist's office building. Another series of shots showed her by her place of work. "She circled five times," Mr. Ahmet indicated, pointing to the digital time stamp in the lower right corner of a series of shots. "She was, no doubt, very troubled."

Mr. Ahmet sifted through more folders, produced a transcript of an interview with the night nurse on the intensive care unit floor where Helen had been transferred. An accompanying security camera shot showed Walter trying to buy coffee from a vending machine. Mr. Ahmet's finger touched the image, Walter undoubtedly a man lost in the world. He tried the vending machine a second time. It was caught in another still. And then there was the disjunctive moment of how the end started, a grainy shot, Walter pointing a gun at the nurse. Mr. Ahmet said quietly, shaking his head, "It was decided in an instant . . ."

A moment passed. Mr. Ahmet took out another folder, unrelated to events on the day of Walter and Helen's deaths. After the original trial and acquittal, the district attorney's office had continued pursuing Walter and the others. There was continued extortion.

Mr. Ahmet said pointedly, "Nothing was ever linked to Walter. Nobody turned evidence on him. I was asked to discreetly verify various rumors. Helen purchased a fur coat for over two thousand dollars at one point. I followed up. A clerk identified her as having paid in cash. There were other purchases, extravagances, a pearl necklace, a limited-edition Montblanc pen. Purchases totaled over $15,000 at a series of department stores. I interviewed Helen. I asked about the fur coat. She denied the purchase. I uncovered a fur care service contract, only offered to those who purchased directly from the store. Her signature was on record. I presented her with it. She had no answers."

Mr. Ahmet shook his head. "I know a liar when confronted with one. It was not, of course, the case with your father. The more we talked, the more I understood he was hiding a secret. He wanted to admit to taking bribes. I asked for names, who he extorted, how much he received. Of course, he could not tell me."

Mr. Ahmet looked up. "You appreciate, it was a difficult situation? I interviewed Helen again. She called me 'the ant,' and I said, '*The ant* will ask you again, Mrs. Price . . .'"

"It was difficult to navigate. Your father was a friend. What I can tell you, your parents were preoccupied with a crisis in their own lives and quite beyond the reach of reason. Regrettably, when two drowning people are locked in a struggle, they will inevitably take each other under. Both will die."

Mr. Ahmet came back to certain points, laying out a sequence of shots taken from camera footage along Lake Shore. He pointed to Walter's unmarked car with its lights flashing, and Helen, a car ahead of him.

A series of shots showed Helen's head turn around before she changed lanes, crossing all six lanes of Lake Shore Drive. Mr. Ahmet pointed to the steering wheel turned in a hand-over-hand maneuver. Helen Price had attempted suicide.

Mr. Ahmet said, staring at the shot, "Maybe, sometimes the secrets we withhold reveal more about us than what we ever say. It is perhaps better understood by greater minds. I am simply a gatherer of evidence." In saying it, he gathered the photographs. On the back of each, a time-line was established, along with grounding facts written in a looping cursive. Helen's scheduled meeting with her oncologist—she had been charged for the no-show.

Mr. Ahmet thumbed through a stash of receipts, photostatic copies of medical preauthorization codes, an electronic life cycle connected with what eventually transpired—Helen's death. The bills, the doctor's office visit, the ambulance EMT, her hospital stay, arrived at over weeks and months, the late payment notices and eventual threats for nonpayment, all were part of a file Mr. Ahmet had gathered. He had tallied the cost, the vast expenditure of how hard it was to die. He had a number circled.

Norman touched the receipts as evidence of a dark existential truth. He imagined a scene, a roll call of amounts, the tally of a figure rising.

After gathering and putting away the files, Mr. Ahmet suppressed an urge to yawn, then yawned. He apologized. It had been a long morning.

Norman cleared his throat and asked, "How might I get a copy of these files?"

Mr. Ahmet touched the box with both hands, moved it an inch or so, perceptibly closer to Norman. "It is yours. There are copies of copies on file." He waited a moment. "I will just ask, tell it honestly, Mr. Price, for them and for yourself."

Seventeen

A GLASS ELEVATOR soundlessly arrived on the floor and opened. Nate stepped out in the tiled expanse of a marbled floor of the law office of Weatherly, Sutherland, and Saunders.

All three lawyers were gathered in an office skyrise with varnished trim, leatherback chairs, and an ornate throw rug. Morning arrived in a resplendent ball of light, reflected in skyscraper windows. The azure of the lake was visible at this height.

A beautiful Latino secretary with almond-shaped eyes greeted Nate and directed him to a waiting room appointed with inlaid shelves and leather-bound books.

The lawyers, in the practice of selling their time, took their collective ease, checking their watches. Nate was ten minutes early, so they waited, and he waited.

Disconcertingly, he saw alongside the framed law degrees, that all three had served in Vietnam, their pictures set against an American flag.

IT HAD TAKEN TIME to track Nate Feldman. The law office had hired a private investigative agency, and it was through documents connected with the sale of Nate's organics business, specifically, the uncovering of an outstanding IRS bill for unpaid capital gains, that led to his being located in Canada. The law office prided itself on its thoroughness and professionalism. The firm had a facsimile of the bill from the IRS and Nate's social security number printed in block lettering.

Weatherly went about handing the facsimile over. Nate had the presence of mind not to take receivership of it. He knew enough about the law.

There was an IRS statute that all American citizens living abroad were required to pay US taxes. Weatherly pointedly asked, "Are you aware of this?"

Nate felt a grave and sudden danger that this had been a grand trap to bring him back to America, though it turned out to be simply Weatherly, Sutherland, and Saunders asserting their collective history. Any of them could have conducted what turned out to be the dull formality of documents that needed his signature. Nate read each document, or pretended to do so, under the gaze of all three, who had come to simply stare him down. He was willing to concede to their service. They were better men.

With the lawyers' departure, the secretary executed the release of the reels. Nate signed a series of forms. As he stood beside her, she might have been an incarnation of Ursula. It struck him, how a life moved through cycles—the realities of what you might have, what you had, and what you would never have again. He might have said it, told her how a beauty like hers shouldn't be cheapened with lipstick, stockings, and heels, how each hid her essence.

Thinking it caused a stabbing pain where it hurt nearly always now.

IN THE GREY DARK of the Drake Hotel room, Nate was inclined to understand how a Holy War—or the idea of a suicide bombing, its conception and then commitment to it—might be sustained by staying in a hotel room, in a bewildering disorientation of postmodern isolation, with a minibar charging six dollars for a bottle of water. He regretted the thought immediately. He was not thinking straight.

He should have left Chicago and not checked into the Drake, but he had done it for a sense of nostalgia; this was where his father and mother had first met. He wanted to show Ursula, let her see it through his eyes.

He was too early to check in. As a courtesy, he was extended the offer to store his luggage. He did so, then went toward a bar in an alcove where his parents first met. His father had taken him there after a day of Christmas shopping, the bar burnished brass railings and leatherback chairs—on the drinks' menu, highball cocktails, old fashioneds, and whiskey sours.

Nate sat alone. A bartender wiped down shelves. Nate ordered a drink in the impropriety of 10 A.M., indicating his room was not available but that he was a guest. The bartender proved no friend. The bar opened at noon. Nate waited in the subterranean murk of the bar. He could see the ankles of people passing in the street above.

At a point, the barman came over and asked if Nate was okay. Nate was apparently talking aloud. He apologized. He announced he had driven down from Canada.

Thereafter, a manager found Nate and determined there was, in fact, a room ready. Nate walked with an awareness that he was old, that it was observable and noted. He had been up since 5 A.M.

THERE WAS THE ISSUE of whether he wanted to review the reels in Chicago or back home. It involved securing a Super 8 projector. He was so very tired. He was undecided, but Ursula advised that he should, for the contiguous sense that all this should unfold here. She was right.

He checked Craigslist. A projector was offered by someone in Chicago. It was done, the search, the bid, the buy, in less than ten minutes. He paid for expedited delivery and received a confirmation notice that it would be there by four in the afternoon.

In the silence, much was lost to him. He should have stayed in Canada, left mystery aside. There was nothing to be gained. He argued with Ursula. His life, the totality of it, had been with her. He could sleep a number of hours, leave the reels here, not take receipt of the projector, leave it all behind. It was an option. He had choices.

He checked to see if Norman Price had responded. He had not. It furthered a disconnect, made less vital whatever it was that had been bequeathed to him.

Everything took on a flatness in the grey dark of drawn curtain. The hotel room hadn't the luxury he had anticipated. The suites with their elegant bar had been swapped out for small refurbished rooms. When he left, there was still the Playboy Mansion and a tacit understanding that certain women might spend their best years in rabbit ears, bunny tails, and heels, toting trays of cigarettes and cigars, and that neither men nor women, for that matter, saw any contradiction, subjugation, or irony in any of it. His father had subscribed to *Playboy*. What he could say was that there was no Playboy Mansion anymore. It had disappeared from the skyline. Not that it was undone, the baser instincts confined now to a rougher sexual content on the internet, anything you could imagine a search word away.

NATE REACHED FOR the blankets, drew himself into a ball on the bed. He felt the smallness of the room around him. He could feel the eyes of the three lawyers in judgment. It had not been easy.

In a summative assessment of life, he felt the need now to press his case. When he arrived in Canada, he had nothing. He recalled it, the memory of desolate places in an early falling snow, miles walked alone. It was not a given that he would survive. The work at the mill had been new to him, but in the act of physical labor he had grown strong, confident. It had set him on an equal footing with those who had worked the mill their entire lives. He took a correspondence course with an agricultural college, extended the reach of what was offered there, sought a greater life, pursued further opportunity. He followed the advice of provincial government pamphlets out of Ottawa, used potash fertilizer as a hold against depleted soil, grew a hardy root crop of beets, rutabaga, yams, sweet potatoes, parsnips, and carrots. He tapped a line of trees for maple syrup, ordered a colony of bees from Prince Edward Island.

Ursula was then at the center of his life, her presence compelling a want in him to do better. They had savings in a jar, wads of bills with the picture of Queen Elizabeth. Ursula baked scones and flat cakes, served them with black tea and honey. She watched him study, Nate conscious of the act of watching her watch him. Their lives grew in a deeper soil.

He recalled the bite of the axe running up along his arms, the centered sense of a life so contained and the hungry mouths of the traps that snapped unseen in the finality of a sudden and merciful end. At night, he worked on his studies by candlelight, Ursula, then pregnant, cautioning him against exhaustion and, at times, spectral as a ghost, blowing out the candle. In the sudden dark, a day ended.

IN A QUIET DELIBERATION of something needing to be finally settled, Nate steadied himself and wrote—*Taking dinner at the Drake at eight this evening. An invitation stands. As ever—NF!*

Eighteen

Joanne was asleep in the makeshift of her tent in the living room when Norman arrived home.

Grace looked up.

Norman set the box down and whispered, "I want to show you something." He took Grace by the crook of his finger. Randolph followed.

In his office, he opened an image of Grace on a fifty-five-cent miniature ice cream truck ride. The shot had been taken at a mall in her first month in America. "That's you when you came to us."

Grace turned earnestly and said, "Me?"

"You." Norman set his chin on the crown of her head. He was crying without sound.

Grace pointed and said, "Randolph, that's me!"

Randolph nosed Norman's leg, reaching Grace's hand.

Upon his return from signing forms related to Norman's release, Mr. Ahmet revealed that Kenneth had attempted to blackmail Saul Herzog. The murder bore the hallmark of a professional hit.

Norman opened another shot. In it, Kenneth was holding Grace, both sitting in a helicopter with Big Bird. Norman zoomed in to see if Grace remembered Kenneth. If she did, she said nothing.

Joanne watched from the doorway. Norman was aware of her presence. He said her name so she understood that he knew.

She came forward, fought a quaver in her voice. She said, "Kenneth left a letter. He was so very sorry. He wanted the money for you and Grace. He took a risk and lost."

Nineteen

DOWN ON THE STREET below his hotel window, Nate could hear the sound of traffic. There were people everywhere. He had lost a certain perspective, an ability to see in the way one loses a sense of depth perception on the tundra. The Eskimo compensated and learned to see the world through a slit in a piece of bone. He was doing it through the split between the blinds. His eyes hurt and adjusted. It was snowing.

On his laptop, Nate turned to a site from the Philippines. You could buy a kidney on the internet. There were testimonies of Western patients. A line of bantamweight men, all with their arms raised, revealed stitch marks running beneath their ribcages, all posed against a Manila slum of corrugated shacks. It had come to this!

IF NATE WAS HONEST, Grandshire was not the Paradise Found it had first seemed but rather a Paradise Lost, for the leach of unseen metal contaminants from the mining of the nineteenth and twentieth centuries—trace elements, zinc, cadmium, lead, manganese, nickel, and arsenic, all released into stream-fed aquifers in old operations lost to the wilderness.

The details were contained in government reports—soil analysis, evidence of contamination sources identified. For the victims, the effects were slow to manifest but pernicious, cumulative, and irreversible, leading to organ failure. Medically and legally, it was a complicated matter. At issue, the absolute causality of the associated illnesses. Lawyers and experts lined up on both sides of the argument, so it was apparent there would be no justice for the immediate victims and little, if any, for surviving family members.

The witnesses were simply called to put a face to a story. This was Ursula's opinion.

Cynicism, she said, was a white disease, and now they were going to add this injury to her end. She would not allow it. She spoke of a mushroom grown in the fetid dark that allowed her people to speak with their ancestors. They should know and be ready for her arrival. Death should be nothing hidden in the palliative care of a hospice on Toronto's outskirts.

It was understood better, she maintained, this cycle, her illness, what had befallen her, by the tribal leaders of old and more recently by men like Frank Grey Eyes—the first indication of disruption registered in the depletion of fish stock and the bitter taste of game when a sickness could slow an animal imperceptibly, but enough so that it was caught, and if caught in too great a number, then the species should be left to recover.

This was generationally observed, these signaling events told in any number of stories of how, in ancient times, the lakes and streams and rivers sometimes churned in the turbidity of waters in a choke-out by a nonindigenous grass or weed, seed carried on the wind so a balance was upset, the soil silted so it was hard for the salmon to find their way and lay their eggs in what had been the clear pooling of once undisturbed waters.

IN THEIR TIME, toward the end, as Ursula faded, Nate added remote and distant histories. He purchased a history of Canada, went to town, stood in the cold vestibule of the post office, and collected books wrapped in a crinkle of brown paper.

Ursula was taken by a new history, the story of Basque whalers, who throughout the sixteenth century had sailed the Americas, more intent on concealing their hunting territory than claiming land, when the bounty of whale oil lit the lanterns of Europe.

In between the facts, in the margins of the book, was the tale of a fisherman who hauled up a three-foot-long cod, common enough at the time. But what was astonishing, the cod spoke an unknown language. It spoke Basque.

Ursula liked the story best, drowsing and waking again. She asked to be propped with a pillow, taking the picture book in her lap, witnessing the Basque whalers in the grey swell and kickup of whitecaps, harpoons at the ready in the heel of a chase, and a page later, the dead-eyed whale, pinioned and hoisted, the men preparing for the quiver and shudder of blubber flensed, the content of a belly left to spill in a great effluence of its precious oily fat.

This, Ursula, believed, was how you lived. She was fascinated at the Basques in the belly of the whale—a leviathan put there by the spirits—sheathing, disassembling a life, its essences harvested and recycled, and believing there must have been much attenuated prayer and ceremony involved in such a profession. Ursula did not shudder from the hunt in the way the environmentalists would have. Their interests were divergent, hers and theirs. They were scared of death. She mistrusted any man who did not have blood on his hands or who had not killed out of necessity and fed his family. If you had not, then you were soft, and your love of nature was deformed.

THE PROJECTOR ARRIVED while Nate slept. A concierge delivered it to the room. It proved a heavy, gunmetal grey contraption with a dead weight not found anymore in objects. Nate set it on a chair. A length of cord ran to a wall socket. A light glowed, and with it a smell of scorched dust showed in a scattered beam.

Nate had the box of reels on the bed. They were in chronological order. He had certain years in his head. He moved the reels accordingly with some calculus of events. He would be lying if he said he didn't know why he had come south again. In Grandshire, on the internet, he had seen pictures of Norman Price, the shared jawline of the Feldman family. He went searching for it not long after the letter arrived from the lawyers. He knew a dark secret was being revealed, one long suspected, Helen Price asserting her hold over the Feldmans. It was how he saw it, a cold indictment passed down, suggesting the sort of woman Helen Price was. He stood in the grey light with the curtains drawn.

The reels had all been recorded at the office. The ones he was interested in were taken post–Norman's birth. The reel turned in static-filled black-and-white, his father stepping into and out of frame, a series of outtakes. There was no sound.

There was the single sequence at a certain date. Nate fed the reel in a blurred advance and arrived at a scene. Helen Price's gloved hand adjusted the lens. She emerged, walking away from the camera, this woman, now dead. Nate held his breath. He cared little about her. She was there in the historical record. To get to his father, he had to go through her.

Helen Price's hair was combed in a wave off her forehead. Her eyes were sunken, suggestive of a period of convalescence, her lips a shade not identifiable in black and white, and yet he observed the exercising control she maintained, an influence and presence that would not be dismissed. It was communed in the quiver of her hold on his father's arm, this the first time Helen Price had appeared alongside his father, his father suffering through it, and left, holding the baby. There were sayings that literal.

It was recorded without sound. It went on longer than it should. His father's lips began moving. He spoke out of the corner of his mouth. He was saying something. It added a solemnity to have his father speak and not hear it.

He remembered far back with Ursula, how she had quieted him on their first night after the act was done. She wanted to hear his heart and not his opinions. Words meant so little as he quietly caved to a love that would sustain them. It was the opposite in this instance, the silence so sharp in the insistence of an underlying rage barely contained.

In releasing the child, there was opportunity for some show of affection. His father was a head taller, his lips near the crown of Helen Price's head. He did not kiss her, though, at one point, there had been an act and an intimacy that begat a child.

Nate stopped the projector as the child was surrendered. In their absence, across the skyline, was a carving of a giant Egyptian and Indian cradling a clock. It was 4:46 P.M. in late April 1963. April 22 to be precise.

Nate checked the historical meteorological records. The mercury sixty-two degrees in what was described as a week of glorious weather, a high-pressure front of blue skies. It was a point of no importance, but a fact, nonetheless. The Cubs were playing well out in the Cactus League in Arizona, in advance of what would be their first winning season since 1946. Jack Brickhouse was making the calls on WGN.

Nate went through more reels. His father wore his pants cinched above the hips. He had a build not dissimilar to Clark Kent, Kent's glasses such a weak conceit, when it was less about Lois Lane being duped than her wanting to be, Lois permitting normalcy to proceed alongside valor as it did in the lives of so many who had served during the war.

Nate fed another spool, unraveling unremitting hours of tedium, his father at his office window, his gaze like some desultory God.

At some point, a tripod was purchased. Helen appeared in one sequence. She sat at his father's desk, paged through files in a way she thought business was conducted. Nate looked at her, thought her so fundamentally ignorant, her misconception of how men of power acted, when she had evidence to the contrary, when there must have been confidences gained and succor sought, before eventually, and without ceremony—like mild-mannered Clark Kent—his father had taken his leave, not up, up and away, but to his death below.

NATE'S CELL PHONE beeped, a declarative one-liner text from Norman Price. *In the lobby.*

A minute passed, then five, then ten.

Theodore Feldman had done Helen Price a great harm. Nate believed it. There was no good that could come in any disclosure. He would spare Norman Price.

Another message arrived, a single word, *Here!*

It had been a mistake summoning Norman Price.

Nate sent a cursory message, abrupt but deferential. *Deepest apologies, due to unanticipated circumstances, returned home!*

PART III

The struggle itself towards the heights is enough
to fill a man's heart. One must imagine Sisyphus happy.

—ALBERT CAMUS

Twenty

THERE WAS "ACTIVITY" on the house, as the realtor described it, a tentative cash offer by a Mexican family who ran a lawn care business; the issue at hand, their legal status. The family had been to the house three times already. There was nothing easy in real estate, and it was made more difficult with the tightening of credit. An intermediary, a legal immigrant, was fronting the offer. It was done within "their" community. The realtor sounded unsure. She had not worked with "these" people before.

Under better market conditions, the house might have been a starter home for a young upwardly mobile couple, the house close to the commuter train.

The realtor warned that the projected tentative offer would be lowball. They had a number in mind. Norman should be prepared to counter. He magnanimously declined. They were hardworking people, and if they could swing it, he wanted the deal closed.

The realtor called on a daily basis. The family wanted to do to a final walkthrough. The realtor advised of further rumblings. Norman should brace for an even lower offer. His only solace, he held no note on the house. The question: How much was he willing to lose in a sale, or how little was he hoping to gain?

AT THE KITCHEN TABLE, Joanne explained the term "recon" to Grace. That was what Joanne was calling the trip out to the house. She posed, James Bond style, her hands clasped, her index fingers extended in the shape of a gun.

Grace ate a waffle drowned in maple syrup. She had not seen James

Bond, but Joanne, undeterred, was determined that Norman play the bad guy.

He obliged and made a cackling, evil laugh, advancing on Joanne, who said, "Do you expect me to talk?"

Norman answering in his best evil voice, "No, Mr. Bond, I expect you to die!"

The spectacle alarmed Randolph, who barked. His legs skated out from beneath him on the tile kitchen flooring.

They were forty-five minutes behind schedule. Norman refrained mentioning it.

Norman packed the dishwasher, then went into the hallway.

Grace looked up at him. She was sitting, earnestly aligning her winter boots. Joanne had put a sticker on each boot, kittens with paws raised, so when aligned properly, the paws completed a heart shape. Grace learning not so much her right from her left but a strategy to complete the task, Norman mindful that the act of communication required one take into account the other's temperament or self-awareness.

THE MEXICAN FAMILY arrived with a trailer of lawn equipment, most notably a wood-chipper. There was no pretense about what they were or how they earned a living, the name Suarez Lawn Care written on the sides of the trailer.

The truck cab had an old-fashioned bench seat. There were three up front, Mr. and Mrs. Sanchez and a grandmother. None wore seatbelts.

A minivan arrived. Another Mexican woman emerged in identical spandex tights and embroidered sweater to Mrs. Sanchez, evidently her sister. They greeted with a kiss.

Joanne circled the block.

A Cutlass Supreme with alloy rims on oversized tires pulled into the driveway.

The realtor arrived ten minutes later in a white Cadillac. She parked behind the woodchipper. She emerged in a bustle of professional importance, carrying a briefcase. Norman looked at her and shouted, "She's going to kill the deal."

Joanne said, "Let her do her job!"

NORMAN WAITED ten long minutes, then exited the car, rang the doorbell to his own house.

The realtor had never actually met him. He identified himself as a drive-by interest and in the market. He pointed to the sign and entered the hall. The realtor seemed on the verge of protesting, but it would have been awkward and disruptive to try explaining it to the Suarez family.

From what Norman could determine, the Suarezes were sold on the house; groups dispersed to various quarters of the house. The furnace was on full blast. The father—Miguel—his name embroidered on his shirt, fiddled with the thermostat. The father communicated a question in Spanish, and the son asked the realtor to see the heating bill.

The Sanchez family didn't care about the formality of a dining room. This had been the single biggest issue for other prospective buyers. Norman watched the father merely look at it and move on.

A voice called from the basement.

The sister-in-law, Mrs. Suarez, and the grandmother were down there.

Norman followed at a distance.

There was a fetid odor of mildew. Mrs. Suarez fanned her nose. The source of the smell was discussed in Spanish, and again a question was relayed to the son, who in turn asked the realtor, who wrote down notes on a sheet attached to a clipboard.

The son tapped the faux wood paneling that had been installed to disguise poorly installed drywall.

In the unfinished laundry room, Norman turned on the only faucet not running in the house, just to show some genuine and competing interest.

The grandmother fingered rosary beads, her mouth moving in a prayer. She said the word "daycare." Seemingly, there was no word for it in Spanish.

The son took out a tape measure and made a series of measurements. The conversation continued, conducted in Spanish, then English when the realtor was questioned.

The realtor was unsure of the legality of commercial zoning. There were ordinances.

Norman refrained from intervening. Across the basement, he could see the crawlspace, mindful of what was still there—his porn magazines.

The basement would become a daycare business, this basement where he had jacked off and where Helen, in her failing years, had watched *Judge Judy*, becoming an expert in small claims cases, fence line disagreements and overhanging trees, Helen affirmed in her belief that you should always take pictures and bring at least two legitimate estimates to court. This had been the end of her days.

The Suarez family moved through a glass door to a patio and garden.

Norman ascended into the upper half of the house. Joanne and Grace were standing outside Norman's old bedroom. In the discharge of an emotion, Joanne pointed at a poster and said, "I would never have pegged you for a Star Wars fan."

Norman answered, "I was in love with Harrison Ford."

He smiled as he said it, and Joanne smiled.

The realtor had done Norman no favors. In his parent's bedroom Helen's medicines were on the counter, a glass of water dried to a hoary calcified coating.

The entire upper floor smelt of antiseptic bandaging and menthol. Norman felt nauseated. In the bathroom, he opened a vent, a fan whirling in a funneling suck of air like the house needed to exhale.

Twenty-one

THE CANADIAN NORTH had long been the province of men like Nate Feldman, men escaping civilization, men understanding that wages were paid through a system of good credit at a company store, so there was little real saving, those who arrived resigned that this was the best it would get. Custom dictated against taking photographs. It was attributed to native superstition, when it was really a détente between authorities with an acknowledgement that banishment there was harder than prison.

Of course, times changed. There were fortunes to be made, a new breed venturing north to exploit Canada's resources, the emergence of fracking, but so, too, the advent of chipboard in a resurgent industry of cheap impermanence, homes fit with faux wood panels, prefab furniture assembled with an Allen wrench, where nothing lasted, this constituting the illusion of progress and an economy.

And yet Canada kept hold of certain values. The provincial governments abided by a quasi-socialist policy, without referencing a rhetoric of compassion, universal health care underwritten because of the oil boom towns of Edmonton and Winnipeg and a Pacific influx of millionaire Hong Kong expatriates to Vancouver, the reach of empire not the curse it was in the heart of London. In Canada, the land was too vast, its isolation, its disconnectedness, its greatest virtue, so all that came before was put in the context that nothing survived. It offset a certain fanaticism. It set human existence against a greater presence.

NATE DROVE ALONG the 401 toward Brampton, waited at a Tim Hortons for the early light, entered the rush of traffic descending on

Toronto, then turned onto the 400, going north, when everybody else was heading south.

This was the cycle of urban life. If there was a great disaster, most would die in their cars. It was a terrible thought, though, if an enterprise could be pitched, a survival camp might attract a strain of people committed to the prophetic destiny of End Times.

He had the specs on a series of cabins around a central lodge, all with fishing rights. He might price the added expense of a hydroplane to deposit avid fishermen at any of a number of lakes, remote and inaccessible, where wranglings of the heart and contradictions were best contemplated and settled alone. It was an old idea, come upon as Ursula lay dying. She had a restlessness of a spirit wanting to go farther north toward the end.

URSULA WOULD NOT HAVE made a very good witness in court. She was a contradiction, or the others made her into a contradiction, when life was more complicated. She was on the Organics logo. It defined her in a way neither she nor Nate understood it would. Nate could be charged with conjuring this innocence, capturing her so, but it was done out of genuine love. She cherished what he saw in her. But it was also why the business succeeded, because of her image, captured in the honesty in which Nate had come upon her so long ago. It was their shared truth, uncomplicated.

But people corrupted it, tied it to opinions and ways of organizing a life. She was the essence of a Truth others sought, so she was a fraud for knowing it and letting it perpetuate, for letting her hair grow longer than it might, for being perhaps too native, trapped in the idea of an idea. They got rich. That was the essence of what befell them, if "befell" was a word you might assign to becoming rich.

They were, in the end, trying to recuperate a hidden and remote Truth known only to them, and not to their daughter, who grew to hate the wild, rejecting the silhouetted figure of her mother, a silhouette that grew to resemble her, so she hated it more and more.

What Ursula said of her daughter was that she suffered from a lack of love. In certain bonds, a child could feel a loss from the strength of a union unavailable to her. It was so with Ursula and Nate.

Ursula spoke of how a mother in the wild will risk her life, give of her sustenance to an offspring, but at a certain point, the bond dissolves and the yearling leaves, or the mother drives it away. It happened with their daughter, but it reflected, in a way, Ursula's own path, her reach for someone beyond the immediacy of her own tribe. There were, Ursula said, discontented Eves among the tribes, women who bore the seed of nations and took up with other tribes. She had done so with Nate. Every generation had such daughters, and they made the world a magical place of convergence; they bridged the divide between tribes.

URSULA'S DEATH took a long time. Despite himself, Nate cried, and it made Ursula angry that he saw in her death an end. She could hear him always if he had the strength to listen and hear her.

Ursula never thought she would die rich. It troubled her. What good was money, what did it represent in the way you might leave behind something woven, a blanket or a basket that might be used and be a touchstone to your craft and skill?

She was not angry with Nate, but something was lost. She was the logo and not the person, and she had let that happen, her alone.

She touched Nate's face. She wanted, again, solace in a study of accumulated history, histories he conceived as important, factual, and literal, because there was a great difference between them, and for this she loved him. He completed a part of the unknown world. A mixing of blood was never troublesome to her people. Throughout the ages, women were sent with early settlers to help with new discoveries, women left to fend for themselves amidst the spirited restlessness of men who had not experienced the company of women in a long time. It was managed somehow. Women could walk as far and carry as much as any man, and in the taking of pleasure, they were not demure or filled with anxiety. They took as much as was given and in the morning resumed their place, and nothing was lost in the act. The great measure of a woman was how long she could walk between resting, just the same as a man, no different out there in the wilderness.

URSULA WANTED TO DIE in the solitude of a single love, close to the roar of a fire and a view of the lake. She reached for Nate's face, her hands, near the end, a collection of sticks, the swan of her neck nodding in a sudden keel and slump of gathering sleep.

She was beset by a thirst at the end. They were advised to drink water delivered in plastic bottles. Ursula refused. She drank from a ladle, from a well that was part of the poison.

Nate saw less daylight, winter upon them. He arose and, braced against the cold, felt a consuming presence of where he was, this Canada, its first origins, its indigenous people, and those who followed, the fur traders and the French missionaries, these ghosts, these preternatural presences, coexisting, but equally subsumed in the vast solitude. They were awaiting her departure and arrival into this other world.

In his arms, she eventually slipped from life, an absence more deeply felt than anything ever gained.

NATE ARRIVED HOME in darkness. He felt the absolute aloneness of life. He turned on the generator in the outhouse. It spluttered in starting. He made a fire, put on coffee, sat in the deadening silence. At some point he fell asleep, awoke, and went toward his bed.

Cold frosted the window in his bedroom. He made a circle in the glass with his sleeve. The moon stared back. The greater part of their life had been spent here, he and Ursula contained and provisioned, their own world organized and managed along a time of plenty and scarcity.

It came as a revelation. The name of the enterprise would be Coureurs de Bois. During Ursula's last weeks, he had read to her about the *coureurs de bois*, wood runners—white men who had taken their wives from the native tribes in what was described as à la *façon du pays*, after the custom of the country.

Nate had read from the journal of a Daniel Harmon, who, describing an ancient wedding contract, put it thus, the groom shows his Bride where his Bed is, and they rest together, and do as long as they can agree among themselves, but when either is displeased with their choice, he or she will seek another partner ... which is law here ...

Ursula had liked the idea very much.

IN THE TIME REMAINING, Nate decided that he would honor Ursula in this new venture, that those who came would learn, among other things, how to make fire, to erect shelter, to survive those first days of chaos and distress. He could see death as an approaching reality, a plague perhaps, some calamity, some natural occurrence.

He had plans for safe routes, meeting places, points of connectedness for a family to convene in Toronto. It would call for an outlay of money, but he had the Organics windfall.

He would preach that it mattered how one accounted for one's days and years, for, though a tree might outlive a man, live a hundred or five hundred years, it did so reliant on wildfires to break open and spread its seeds or the wind or the pollination of bees. Fate was a thing decided for a tree, whereas a man could just up and leave—this, why God had ordained the years were so much shorter for humans, the decisions more pressing and urgent.

He would begin with the stabbing hurt of mortality, knowing, at all times, not a minute should be wasted. He would rely on the benevolence of a car crash victim. He would ask Ursula to watch the roads, like an eagle soaring above, for what might be scavenged—the fate of one, an organ donor. It was gruesome, no doubt, but less so than what was on offer in the Philippines.

Twenty-two

YOU COULD FORSAKE sexuality or sublimate it to a point where it mattered less and less. It happened eventually, the great suburban experiment and the associated purchase of so damn much—washers and dryers and home appliances—the essential lure and eventual containment, so you turned to your side of the bed, seeking the escape of sleep, wondering what had become of your youth, your passions and great expectations.

Norman didn't believe in the Kinsey Report, the swapping out of a politics of economics for a politics of sex, which, in his opinion, was part of the great distraction of late modernity. As for his sexuality, he would watch out that he didn't end up strangling kittens, or whatever was said went on in the minds of the sexually repressed or the sexually confused.

He told Joanne about the kittens, to be on guard. She shook his hand, like a deal struck. She had been through enough, understanding that warranties and marriages weren't worth a damn, not in the way they used to be, and honesty, as rare a commodity as gold.

THEY WERE ON A LONG, meandering journey south toward Florida and Disney World. It was planned according to a strict budget. Norman ceded Joanne control of the purse strings, since in the later stages of the house negotiation, she had insisted she could do better—and did. She came out eight thousand dollars ahead of the Suarezes's so-called final offer, holding fast, the great secret to negotiating not fixating on your concerns but assessing what the other side lost in walking.

Heading to Disney World, they ventured into the southern reach of Illinois, where Kenneth was buried.

Norman mapped the trip. He kept the detour a secret.

They were there in just over four hours. Norman drove through a series of abandoned storage buildings along a curve of river.

Grace said, "Daddy, I have to go."

Norman viewed her in the rearview mirror and said, "OK, sweetie."

Joanne, asleep, her mouth half open, roused and, yawning, livened to where they were, so far off the highway. She looked at Norman. He declined to admit why they were there. He said, "We should get gas. And Grace has to go. Right?"

Grace said earnestly, "I got to go, Joanne."

Joanne conceded to the moment and the occasion, saying, "We can stop if you want."

Norman answered, "This is good."

At an intersection, a pickup with bench-style seating pulled alongside, a rifle mounted across the rear cab, a hunting dog, facing straight ahead, sentinel beside its owner. It accounted for a way of life.

At the gas station where Kenneth had worked was a faded poster offering a reward for information leading to the arrest and conviction of those responsible.

Joanne and Grace used a toilet out back. It required a key that hung from a hubcap.

Grace came back and, showing it to Norman, said, "Hicksville!"

Joanne feigned exasperation, while Grace, looking between Norman and Joanne, said, "She said it, Daddy!" pointing at Joanne.

Norman said, "Joanne's right! That's what this is, Hicksville."

THEY WERE ACROSS the Kentucky border. Norman tuned the radio to an AM station. He came upon the last of the spring baseball games played in the Arizona Cactus League.

It stalked him, that old life. He recalled a lazy afternoon long ago, Walter drinking cold beer, mowing the lawn, catching the tail end of a game on a small radio. What Walter loved was the teams in their knickers and stockings, the antiquated side of it, when heroes like Babe Ruth were still revered, despite how Babe looked like a big-diapered baby, but he had delivered on what was asked, swung at dreams, led the way toward manhood with a trot around the bases, his cap tipped, reverent and appreciative of the applause.

It was there again. Walter calling the Cubs "bums," the pennant race lost early, his relationship with them contentious, and yet he had stuck with them out of loyalty, attentive to the line drives, the walks, the loaded bases and the sacrifice fly—the fly a play that smacked of political gamesmanship—the assumption that, under certain circumstances, you might be asked to sacrifice for the team, and that a quirk in the scorecard, in the very game itself, might protect you and allow you to keep the sheet clean.

THEY STAYED AT a schoolhouse turned historic hotel in the heart of coal mining country in Tennessee, their bedroom a converted classroom with high polished floors and tall windows.

It rained in sheets throughout the night. They slept in, awaking into oblong shadows in the billow of a lace curtain, the air clean with a smell of spruce and pine.

Joanne went down to a communal kitchen and began a late morning breakfast.

Norman rose and looked at Grace, kissed her, and let her sleep.

Joanne smiled at his appearance. He wanted to help.

Joanne had it handled. She raised her hand. She was wearing Helen's wedding ring. It was agreed that it made things less complicated if people saw it on her finger. Joanne's hair was flat against her head in an unadorned plainness, theirs a life that would be decided over days, weeks, months, and years, better understood in looking back on what had been decided and not voiced.

Norman indulged and poured cheap, screw-top wine into a tumbler. He said, "Like on the continent, wine with breakfast."

Joanne smiled. "I'm all for decadence . . ." She gulped it down, indicating she wanted a refill.

They were in for the afternoon, locked in shadows.

Grace appeared in Princess Jasmine pajamas. She had found a Scrabble board. Joanne obligingly played while she cooked. They played for pennies.

Norman wandered. In a small library, he came across clothbound books, threadbare with age, a library containing Joseph Conrad's *Heart of Darkness*, Hemingway's *The Old Man and the Sea*, and Jules Verne's *Twenty Thousand Leagues under the Sea*. He looked through a porthole window, saw a church, and beyond, the entrance to the mine, intuiting what an education had offered to those who could make a living above ground, what a powerful inducement it was to study, to see a hole consume and disgorge human life, to study against concussive blasts that regrettably took so many.

Across the way from the schoolhouse hotel was a bronze statue of a miner wearing a hardhat with a miner's lamp. Norman walked out to it. A plaque detailed a mining history linked to labor unrest. The miner was gripping a pick with a strength little needed anymore, though it put into perspective how protective a class of men had been in their collective solidarity to ensure dignity and a living wage. He felt it, a sense of what was again needed.

They were gone the following morning, time collapsing in a run of mile markers and states crossed, a flinty brilliance of coastal light replacing the dappled lace of forest canopy.

CAPTAIN CODY'S outside Daytona had an All-U-Can-Eat seafood salad bar buffet done as a sandbar, the restaurant's namesake, Captain Cody, a grizzled plaster cast with disconcerting blue doll eyes, who, every so often, said, in a cragged English accent, "Ahoy, Matey," this all miraculously conjured daily for $7.95!

Norman was sure Captain Cody's was tied to a medical conglomerate, these cheap eats underwritten in the greater trawl of monies associated with geriatric end-of-life care, everything else here the lure: the sun, the palm trees, the beach, and the sunsets.

There was no great hurry. The tickets to Disney were for the following day. They whiled away almost two hours. The sun grew in intensity until the asphalt wavered.

Norman regretted having declined valet parking, with the reflexive opinion it was a great trap, when tipping was at one's discretion, and the service that much better for there being no set charge, no social front-loading of fees or hidden taxes. It was how they liked it down here. You were underwriting nobody else. Individual rights remained intact.

There were refills on the refills on refills, or that's how Joanne described it, rising and coming back with another Pepsi in a beaded goblet, like pirate booty.

Toward the end of lunch, a garish fluorescence killed the tropical mood. Two waitresses, on break, smoked in a booth. Grace eyed Captain Cody. He was a great source of curiosity. The waitresses got a kick out of watching Grace, while another waitress in her sixties, some castaway beauty of pageants, a one-time mermaid who had not fared so well on land, hosed the crushed ice, so the magic that had been a sandbar was eventually gone.

Norman took his time, observing and writing everything on napkins to the amusement of Joanne, who wanted to see what he was writing.

Norman shielded it, saying, "You'll read about it eventually."

Joanne eyed a dessert, a key lime pie beached on the sandbar not yet fully cleared.

She bolted. Norman watched. He was a man with a singular interest still, with no other apparent qualities, and yet Joanne, for her part, was satisfied that between them, they would see this through in the apportioning of civility and good manners. This was not discounting love. It was just arriving at it in a way that was out of fashion, when time and understanding were most often what was needed.

In her absence Norman felt what aloneness might feel like again. He looked out on the wavering heat. It seemed like the continuation of one long life really. Florida had been an abiding dream of his father's, a retirement here discussed, so he had a scenario in his head that his parents were, in fact, down here. It wasn't hard to imagine. There had been no closure, no ceremony. He had just not seen his parents in a long time.

Joanne returned with some brochures. They might go down along the coast for a cruise to catch the sunset later. The brochures guaranteed sightings of manta rays. Their AAA card guaranteed 10 percent off all listed prices.

Norman let her manage it. He would get on whatever boat he was told to get on.

Joanne eventually got the check, peeling her legs from the sweat of the vinyl seating. She suggested that they all use the bathroom in a testament to all-things practical. Meanwhile, Norman stared at Grace, who was preoccupied with Captain Cody in a quiet investigation of his mystery.

Joanne helped look for where the sound was coming from, asking questions, leading Grace, who was intelligent and beautiful and in the care of Norman Price, her father.

NORMAN HAD followed up on Nate Feldman, in the enigma of his sudden return to Canada. He texted on a number of occasions, heard nothing, then uncovered Nate Feldman's online obituary. His body was discovered in state of predation. He died cutting wood. He had been in the end stages of kidney failure, medical complications related to alleged water contamination by legacy mining operations close to his property. The case was in the courts, in a protracted battle of legal motions.

There was reference to Nate's wife, Ursula. She, too, had passed, due to cancer, and was named in an ongoing suit against a number of mining operators and the provincial government. There was an inset picture of her. She was arrestingly beautiful. Her silhouette had graced the logo of the successful organics business she and Nate had owned.

A week later, Weatherly, Sutherland, and Saunders contacted Norman. Nate Feldman had bequeathed him a set of film reels and a projector. It was not formally disclosed how Nate came into the reels' possession, but when Norman went to the law office to collect them, a secretary informally revealed that they had been bequeathed initially by Helen Price to Nate Feldman.

Norman watched the reels alone, came across the first time that he was held by Mr. Feldman, who looked like King Solomon tasked with deciding whose child this was. It changed little, or he was determined it shouldn't. Walter Price was his father. What he thought of his mother, well, his feelings were less generous.

NORMAN CONTINUED to watch Grace follow a cord that connected from the wall to the lumbar region of Captain Cody. She pulled at it, found an opening to a small metal box.

She said excitedly, "I found it, Daddy!"

Norman smiled, imagining again what a reconciliation might have been like with his parents. Walter caught up in a generational entanglement of new worries, wading through the new economy of geriatrics teeming with predatory financial advisors trawling the pension funds of former union zealots turned conservative, now united against a welfare state intent on supporting bums, one-time union retirees submitting to the sway of latter-day Tea Party conservatives, calling for moral accountability, tough love, and lower taxes.

He closed his eyes. Yes, Walter and Helen living in a trailer park with a low-maintenance pea gravel lawn, their life aligned with the last of the greatest generation, patriots turned scrupulous coupon cutters, a rear guard aged who had seen their influence extended in the hanging chad debacle that determined the course of a new imperialism, emboldening the then would-be 9/11 hijackers logging their flight class hours along the Florida Panhandle.

It was not come to terms with fully, even yet, the great wound of 9/11. He had seen it on bumper stickers through so many states. At play in the collective consciousness, in a country where God was asked to confer his blessing, bags had been packed, wives and children kissed, cabs hailed, and all dying before the in-flight service began. Though the stories told now were not those stories but invariably the outlier stories of those who woke up too late, the late connection, the hangover, those without upgrade points. In these isolated stories of survival, Jesus's mercy was made known, not so the improbable sequence of actual events that got the rest to their appointed death with the assuring sense in their hearts that, on that day, there was a God watching over them and determining their destiny all along.

THEY MADE A DASH across the furnace of the shimmering asphalt to their rental, to the delight of two loitering parking attendants. The car roiled in a wave of heat.

Joanne had on Jackie Onassis sunglasses. Norman saw just her smile and not her eyes. Yes, they should have paid the dollar for parking. All life was not a scam.

Out back of Captain Cody's, a screech of birds hung over two bus-boys emptying a slush of leftovers. A pelican, its wingspan immense in arresting flight, landed, its low-hung belly like a transport carrier. The busboys fed it a flotsam of shrimp, crab leg, oyster, pot roast, all manner of salads, beets, and slaws. Then the pelican, in a waddling gait, crossed the scorch of asphalt, seeking flight.

Buoyed on an uplift of unseen thermals, an indiscernible aerodynamics was made apparent, the tuck of head and spread of wings, so this creature might go for a long time over the ocean caps, Norman Price made mindful of what might be achieved on the right thermal, with the right attitude, and aware that he was riding such a thermal and in the midst of great flight.